An Elephant's Journey
Thunder IV
Tusker

Erik Daniel Shein
Melissa Davis

Though inspired by true events, this book is a work of fiction. The characters, incidents, and dialogues are products of the author's imagination and are not to be construed as real. Any resemblance to actual events or persons, living or dead, is entirely coincidental.

World Castle Publishing, LLC
Pensacola, Florida
Copyright © 2018 Arkwatch Holdings, LLC, and Erik Daniel Shein
Co-Author: Melissa Davis
Hardback ISBN: 9781629898032
Hardback Collector ISBN: 9781629897745
Paperback ISBN: 9781629897752
eBook ISBN: 9781629897769

First Edition World Castle Publishing, LLC, May 14, 2018
http://www.worldcastlepublishing.com

Licensing Notes
Requests for information should be addressed to:
Arkwatch Holdings, LLC
4766 East Eden drive
Cave Creek, AZ 85331
Cover: Arkwatch Holdings, LLC and Karen Fuller
Cover Art Animation: Lenord Robinson
Illustrator: Paul Barton, II
Editor: Maxine Bringenberg

Table of Contents

CHAPTER 1
HIDE AND SEEK

Birds twittered in the trees above as fingers of light splashed through the green leaves shimmering in small lines on the ground. A tiny blue morpho caterpillar named Katerina was munching on an elephant ear in such large gulps she barely inhaled any air. The leaf shook slightly and she glared at the intrusion.

"Hey! I'm eating here!"

"Oh, sorry," a small elephant called up to her.

"Quiet, T.J., or they'll find us." Julian, a small plated lizard, poked him on the back with the tip of his tail. He was perched on top of the elephant's head, peering out from the side of the tree.

Thunder Junior, an African pygmy elephant, was playing a game of hide and seek with his friends.

5

They rarely called him Thunder, due to the fact that his father had the same name. When he was first born, the elephant calf's stomp was just as loud the roaring thunder above. This was a trait that he shared with his father, Thunder, which was why he had the same name. He still responded to Thunder, but for the most part he had taken to the nickname his friends had given him. His parents still called him Junior, often making him feel like a baby. Even though he was still a young elephant, he did not want to be treated like a baby.

"Right…sorry." His whisper was so quiet only the mouse crouching nearby seemed to take notice. He stopped scrounging in the dirt underneath him and wrinkled his nose at T.J. before going back to his scavenging.

"Ears up, T.J. Here comes Copper," Julian cautioned him.

T.J. was hiding behind a large tree. It barely covered any of him, and try as he might he could not get his sides to squish in enough to conceal himself. Not that it mattered though. Copper was an African grey parrot with very poor eyesight. When the bird started to approach the tree, T.J. held his ears up straight at the sides of his head and pretended to be leaves sprouting from the tree.

"Yoohooo! Where are you?" the parrot called out. He circled around the forest a few times before landing on a small boulder nearby. "Helloooo?"

T.J. giggled slightly, and Julian pulled at one of the hairs that popped out of the folds of his skin. "Shush!"

When T.J. swatted at him with his trunk, the lizard went flying through the air. He landed on the ground behind him, barely stopping at the base of the plant below. The caterpillar above him held on for her life as the leaves shimmied back and forth. Shaking her head at the pair of them, Katerina grumbled to herself. Then she inched to the corner of the leaf and started to chow down again.

T.J. looked back at Julian and giggled again. "Sorry, Julian!"

Upon hearing the laughter, Copper flew into the air and examined the tree closely. The parrot closed one eye, as if it would make the other work better. "Hmm…. Where is that elephant?"

A small bug flew onto T.J.'s trunk. His eyes crossed as he tried to see what it was. The bug started to wriggle down the length of his trunk, and its tiny legs tickled him with each step. As the bug moved to the tip, T.J. felt a sneeze working its way out. He scrunched his trunk shut and tried to hold it off. The more the bug moved, the harder it was to avoid the itchy feeling crawling through the nasal passageways. T.J. held every muscle in his body as tight as he could, making a last-ditch effort to stay still, but he could no longer fight it. Two things happened at once. A loud sneeze erupted from his trunk, and a loud trumpet sound came from his rear.

"Oh my…that's just…." Julian sat up and tried to wave away the wafting gas that ripped through the air. The lizard got woozy as he inhaled the stench, and fainted to the ground.

"What did you eat? For the love of…." The caterpillar on the leaf looked over at T.J. in alarm as her eyes started to water. Katerina tugged at the leaf and tried to roll it around herself to make a tiny shelter to protect her from the smell that saturated the air. She glared at T.J. from the small holes she had chomped through the leaf. "Can't I just eat in peace?"

T.J. blushed slightly, and his front legs came together in front of him as he apologized. "Sorry!"

"Ah-ha! Found you!" Copper flew over to T.J.'s back and sat down. He looked at the collapsed lizard on the ground and tilted his head in confusion. "What's wrong with him?" The parrot sniffed the air and coughed a little. "Did I do that?"

"No, Copper. That was T.J.!" Julian called up from the ground. Putting his hands up like a corpse reanimating, he pulled himself up and walked like a zombie toward T.J., and stopped just before his friend. "Seriously, we need to put a cork in you."

"Or he needs to eat his veggies." Thunder's mother Kumani ambled slowly over to them, followed by his father Thunder.

"Mom! I hate tubers! I'd rather have fruit."

"Junior, listen to your mother." Thunder's eyes narrowed on his son, even though he was having trouble keeping his face straight. Thunder was often entertained by his son's antics.

"T.J., Dad! Don't call me Junior. Ugh!" T.J. stomped on the ground in frustration. His foot slammed down so hard the trees started to shake.

The black and yellow caterpillar who had been rolled up in the leaf came hurtling to the ground. Katerina landed in a tiny heap and dust kicked up around her. She coughed and sputtered for a moment as the dust attached to the fur around her face. Then she stood up on her back legs and used her tiny leg to make a fist up at him. "Why I oughta!"

None of them seemed to take notice of the

caterpillar as they started to move away from the tree. Katerina crossed her legs in front of her and her face contorted in anger, before a small drop of moisture formed near her eye. Her bright black and greenish yellow body was covered in red and white fluff in odd places that made her look slightly comical and often the butt of other animals' jokes, as well as a voracious eater who stuffed her emotions down with more food than most caterpillars could handle. She crawled closer to a plant and started to shimmy her way back up before she disappeared from sight.

Kumani moved closer to T.J. and put a loving trunk on his head. "Time to go to the water hole, my child."

"Pass!" Julian called up to her. He shuddered slightly. "I hate swimming."

"You could still watch," T.J. suggested.

"Nah, I'm going to go scrounge up some food."

"Your loss," T.J. teased him. He followed after his mother and father.

Thunder turned to his son and smiled. "You know, I once pretended to be a tree."

"I know, Dad! Ugh." T.J. rolled his eyes. "When Frederick helped you get over the fence to find your herd."

"Don't roll your eyes, T.J. It's important to know the past. You never know when it could happen to you," Thunder cautioned him. When he was T.J.'s age poachers had separated him from his mother, sending him on the adventure of a lifetime. His whole life was forever changed by that one moment. He never wanted his son to learn the same mistrust of the uprights, but it was better to be safe than sorry. In a better world, Thunder would never have to worry about that. Their world was changing, but not fast enough to make a dent in the death of other animals like themselves. The only thing they could do was educate their young to keep themselves as safe as possible.

As if noticing his father's dark thoughts, T.J. moved closer to him and put his head against his side. "Sorry, Dad."

Thunder hugged him closer and smiled. "Last one to the water hole is a monkey's uncle!"

"Wait...what?" Copper tilted his head in confusion as he flew above them. "How can an elephant be a monkey's uncle?"

"Just go with it, Copper!" T.J. picked up speed and zipped through the forest. The elephants made their way there in good time, filled with loud panting breaths and giggles as they raced along.

CHAPTER 2
KIDS!

The forest was filled with the chitter chatter of birds as they gossiped about their day. One great blue turaco named Riki bobbed its head back and forth in excitement. Its bright blue feathers were offset by the short cropped plumage on its head with its buzz-cut shape. The turaco paused to watch the elephants approach the water hole. He turned to a hornbill near him. "Is that Thunder?"

Cosmo, the hornbill, gave him a quizzical stare. "You're not from here, are you?"

"No, but I heard the great Thunder lived near here. That's why I came." Riki shifted his feet, one after the other, as the excitement took over.

"He's just an elephant." The hornbill rolled his eyes at the turaco.

13

"Perhaps, but he single-handedly took down the uprights who were poaching from Hope Haven. My mom came from there." Riki stepped to the edge of the branch and watched the trio pass underneath.

"It wasn't single-handed. I heard it was a group effort. See that lion, there?" Cosmo pointed across the waterhole to where Razor was lounging near the water.

Riki looked to where Cosmo directed, and his eyes nearly popped out of his head. "A lion? An actual lion? Wow, there aren't many of those around here. And there's four of them?"

"Well, yeah. That's Razor and his offspring."

"Shouldn't they be with their mother?" Riki crossed his wings over his body as he tried to figure out the quandary before him.

"Well, don't all mothers need a break?" Cosmo pointed out. "I know I sure drove my parents crazy."

Riki nodded his head. "That's probably true. Do you suppose I can meet him?"

"Thunder?" Cosmo looked at him like he had lost his mind. "If you wait a while it will be safer. Once they get in the water, it's a good idea to stay away."

"Why?" The turaco tilted his head and peered closer at the water hole. As the elephants entered the water all kinds of chaos erupted around them. They elephants gathered water in their trunks and started to shoot at anything in their path. Riki barely missed the droplets that soared near him.

"Told you. Those elephants love their water. I'd talk to them when they were on dry land if I were you."

"Right." Riki sat on the tree and waited.

Down below, T.J. was spraying his mother Kumani with water. She sunk her trunk into the water and retaliated in kind. T.J. tried to duck out of the way, but he was drenched by a torrential downpour from her spray. He held up his trunk. "Uncle! Uncle!"

"Did somebody say uncle?" Razor was now standing at the top of the boulder near him. He grabbed onto a vine with his forepaws and swung through the air. "Cannonball!!!"

His splash drenched every animal near him. He came up from the water with a huge toothy grin plastered on his face. Having recovered from his previous injury, Razor was a much happier and active lion. "Come on down, you two."

Two small cubs peered down at them with anxious eyes. Their older sister stood behind them, shaking her head in disgust. "Wimps!"

"If you're so brave, you do it!" Rafa challenged her. The tiny male cub was still shivering at the thought of soaring through the air.

Naya sniffed in irritation. She was trapped between two worlds, the world of a child and that of an adult. Her attitude was that of a grungy teenager who did not want to listen to anyone, or watch after juveniles. "If you don't go, I'm going to push you."

"Fine. I'll go. Boys are such wimps." Zoya rolled her eyes at her brother. Reaching up for a vine, she grabbed onto it just like her father. She zipped through the air on the vine and landed right next to Razor, who now had just shook the water out of his mane. It was now plastered to his head, but he did not seem to mind.

When Zoya came up from the water she called up to her brother. "You coming or what?"

Rafa's nose wrinkled and he gave a slight snarl at his sister. He turned to look at Naya, who was grooming her paw. Seeing no encouragement from her, he glanced down at the water. He gulped loudly as he mentally calculated the distance from the rock down to the water. Taking a deep breath, he grabbed onto the first vine he could get his paws on.

As he started to swing a loud hiss erupted above

him. "Excu-sssssssssssss-e me! Do you mind?"

Rafa's eyes grew large when he found he was swinging from the length of an African rock python. Rafa squealed in fear and his paws released the snake midflight. He flailed through the air with his paws splayed wide open before he hit the cold water below him. When he came up, he spouted water from his mouth and shuddered in revulsion.

His sister rolled onto her back and floated as loud hooting giggles echoed from her lips. She laughed so hard she started to sink into the water. Rolling back to her stomach, she swam to Razor and climbed on his back. "Did you see that, Papa? A snake."

Razor's laughter was joined by the elephants near them. He looked up at Naya and winked, but his daughter rolled her eyes. "You coming down, Naya?"

"You must be dreaming, old man!" Naya plopped down on the rock in almost defiance.

Thunder moved closer to the lion who had become his best friend over the years. "Teens."

"That's the truth. One day you're looking at one tiny face who thinks you lasso the moon. The next, they are treating you like you're chopped liver. We just can't win."

"At least we have a little more time before Junior's in the same boat."

T.J.'s ears perked up at the mention of his name. "Daaaaaaad! It's T.J.! Gahhhhh!"

Razor tilted his head to the right and looked up at his friend. "Looks like it's not that far away."

"Shoosh! You two!" Kumani scowled at them. "Just because I'm expecting our second doesn't mean this one isn't still my baby."

Kumani moved closer to T.J. and started to groom him with her trunk. He pulled away from her in disgust. "Mom!"

The cubs, who were now drying themselves on the bank, started to giggle at him. "Look at T.J.! He still gets groomed," Rafa teased him.

"Yeah! We can already groom ourselves," Zoya agreed.

T.J. put his trunk in the water and sprayed the cubs relentlessly. They now looked like nearly drowned cats, as their fur was plastered to their sides. He smirked at them and chuckled to himself. "Groom that!"

"T.J.! That wasn't very nice!" Kumani chided him.

"But Mom!" T.J. let out an irritated groan.

"Your mother knows how important it is to have good friends in your life. It is only with my friends that I learned to survive. Gather around, everyone." Thunder climbed out of the water and waited for the animals to come closer. He often told the others about his adventures with his friends. Thunder looked around him and saw Riki perched nearby. "Well, hello there. You're new here."

"Why yes...yes, I am. And you are the great Thunder, chosen by the Great Tusker in the sky to bring harmony between the uprights and all mankind, right?"

"I suppose that's true. But not all uprights. You see, there are those that see us as a source of income. And then there are those that are our friends," Thunder answered him.

"But how do you know the difference?" Riki was clearly intrigued.

"You must trust your instincts and surround yourself with those that you trust. I always say that, right Junior?"

T.J. rolled his eyes. "Yes. And when you're in trouble to ask for help."

"That's right. And that's what we did." Thunder started to tell them about his first group of friends.

How the cantankerous rhino and her loyal egrets had helped lead him home. When Copper squawked from above, he included the parrot's mother, Penelope, who would always have a special place in his heart. He spent the rest of the afternoon telling the animals of his journey and what he had learned along the way. If these stories could help another living being remain safe from harm, then the time would always be well spent.

CHAPTER 3
TUSKER'S IN TROUBLE

In the great savanna, far from his home, a giant tusker elephant grazed in the grasses around him. His mate, Thandi, was across the clearing. His ears flapped against his side, shooing the flies from his sensitive skin. A large egret sat on top of him, eating up the bugs that flew too close to him.

Tusker was one of the last of his kind. A natural descendant of the Great Tusker that looked down on the earth below, Tusker lived up to his name. His large ivory tusks pushed away from his face, and were so long they ran parallel to the ground below him. They were a heavy load to bear, not just from their size, but because they made him a target to the world around him. Natural predators were obsessed with him, as killing off a great tusker would bring them a higher social status among the other predators. But these animals were not nearly as dangerous as the ones that walked on two legs. The uprights, men who traveled the countryside hoping to find a creature such as he.

Tusker sighed aloud. He was lucky to have made it this far. Tusker had already outlived most of his blood line, having lost many of his family to the cruel uprights that refused to let them be.

"What's wrong, old man?" Samson called down to him.

"I grow weary of the fight," he answered. And it was true. Tusker would much rather live in a world where he did not have to watch his back around every turn. This fear was the same reason he stayed several paces away from his herd. The distance provided a slight buffer. He was still close enough to see his beloved Thandi and the others.

"Pshaw! You are long for this world, Tusker. Your time isn't nearly up yet." Samson lifted his claws and started to scratch between his feathers.

"My body doesn't move the way it used to, Samson."

"Yes, but your heart is true." Samson flew down to the ground and nibbled up one of the bugs at

23

Tusker's feet.

"You always were a wise bird." Tusker pulled a blade of grass up from the ground and held it closer to his eyes. "Such a simple thing. A blade of grass. So abundant and fresh. The earth provides and we return to it."

"What are you going on about?" Samson flew up and grabbed the blade from his trunk. "It's just a piece of grass."

"I'm just questioning life, Samson. Why we do what we do, how the world runs in cycles around us. There must be some meaning to it all."

"You seek a higher purpose?"

"Always...." Tusker looked up at the sky and wondered what the Great Tusker would think of his life. Had he served a purpose great enough for his ancestor?

"You're a better man than me. All I care about is food." Which was pretty true. Samson came and went often, only returning when his belly rumbled in hunger.

At that moment, a loud screech could be heard in the distance. Some creature was in pain. Tusker used his feet to rumble a message to his mate. He did not want her anywhere near the disturbance. And while he wanted her to move away with the others, his curiosity pulled him closer. He was not surprised to find Samson had taken off the moment the cry erupted. Tusker saw the herd moving away from the sound and his ears opened wide near his head. If he heard it again, Tusker would head for the sound.

"Help!!!" The creature called out for help, and Tusker did the only thing he knew how to do. He ran as fast as his creaking bones would carry him. Someone needed help, and Tusker knew that very few would rise to the occasion. Especially with the uprights taking over more of the savannas.

Tusker turned toward the sound in hopes that he could help the poor soul behind the cries. If it was a predator, Tusker could flash his tusks and chase them off. His tusks had always come in handy that way. He moved as quickly as his tired body could carry him. When he crossed over a small hill, he saw an African sea eagle caught in a nasty little trap. Tusker walked toward the bird, who was struggling inside the metal cage.

"Hold still, I'll try to break you free," Tusker called out to him.

"Careful! The uprights might come back at any moment," the eagle cautioned him.

"I'll be quick then." Tusker used his trunk to feel around the cage. When he found a latch on the other side, he squeezed the tips of his trunk around the latch and pulled as hard as he could. When it gave way, the door swung open and the bird hopped out.

"Thank you very much. I'm Gamba."

"My pleasure, Gamba. I'm Tusker."

As the eagle perched on a branch nearby, a loud hoot and holler came from the grasses nearby from a handful of uprights hiding in the tall blades. Tusker felt every nerve ending start to fire at once as adrenaline pumped through his veins. Uprights this close in the savanna was never a good thing. "Go, Gamba!"

The bird rose up into the air. "Run, Tusker!"

"Save yourself, Gamba. Please, find Thandi and warn her," Tusker called up to him.

"I will, Tusker, but you better fight."

"With everything I've got," he answered him. Tusker watched him fly off and said a prayer to the Great Tusker in the sky for his herd's safety. When the uprights stood up from the grasses, Tusker charged at them with as much veracity as he could muster. His tired limbs moved as fast as they could. He aimed his tusks at one of the uprights that was closest to him, but he did not get very far. Something sharp bit him in the behind and he roared loud in protest. Tusker continued forward, but his mind turned hazy, and he stumbled over his feet as he lost control over his muscles. Tusker crashed in a heap right before his target, and his eyes drifted open and shut a few times before he saw nothing but the darkness of sleep.

CHAPTER 4
GAMBA'S QUEST

The uprights approached Tusker with caution. Just because they had toppled the giant did not mean he would not awake and defend himself. This one was older, but even so it was better to be safe than sorry. One wound could change a man's career path in a matter of moments, especially for poachers. The danger never outweighed the potential profit from their kills.

"Careful, Berko. You don't want to damage the property." Cayman was envisioning dollar signs as he ran a hand along the side of the elephant. He eyed the other man as he jerked the chains around the legs of the giant tusker.

"I still don't see why we can't just take the tusks. They're worth plenty of money, and would be much

29

less trouble to manage."

"That may be, but this collector is willing to pay more than we'd make in a lifetime."

"What does he want with him?" Berko finished shackling the feet and stood back to eye their work.

"Who cares? As long as we get paid."

Cayman barely acknowledged the other men who approached them. They brought their team of elephants that they had trained to follow their every command. These elephants would help lead the tusker through the savannas and make their way to the port where the American had arranged for transport. It would be a long journey, but the payout would be worth it.

"Keep them near. He'll wake up soon enough. We'll break for now," Cayman ordered. No one seemed to question his commands. Cayman was not one they wanted to cross. He was a hardened man who'd fallen on hard times long ago. When he found his way into a group of poachers, he had learned their trade and become one of the most well known in his field. While the officials were onto him, they could never find enough evidence to bring him in. Cayman was too good for that. He had been trained by one of the best, after all.

***

Gamba circled in the sky high above, his eyes trained on the ground below. He had promised to find Thandi, but he needed to see that his new friend was all right. When the uprights brought down the mighty tusker in one fell swoop, he felt his heart sink to the bottom of his stomach. "Oh no...."

The eagle landed in a tree nearby, keeping his eye on the uprights. He felt the need to witness the end of this majestic creature. It was his fault that Tusker had come to this end. If the brave elephant had not come to rescue him, he would not be in this position. Gamba watched as the uprights approached him, and prepared himself for the gruesome end that was about to come.

When the poachers brought shackles forward, Gamba was confused. He had never seen poachers leave an elephant's ivory intact. They seemed to take great care with the creature below. Gamba landed as close as he could, hoping to hear what the uprights were talking about.

Something was off for sure. These uprights had a plan that Gamba did not quite understand. All he knew was Tusker had asked him to warn the others. He might not be able to help him, but the longer he waited here, the more risk there was to the other elephants. If their ivory ran as deep as Tusker's they would be targets for sure. Gamba leapt into the air and flapped his strong wings as hard as he could. He did not even bother to see if the uprights saw his ascent. He had one goal: to find Thandi and the others.

Gamba soared high in the air, making his rounds through the sky until he saw a group of elephants that seemed to be actively traveling in the opposite direction. He flew down lower and called out. "Does one of you happen to be Thandi?"

"She's up ahead," a young elephant answered him. He was running as fast as his legs would carry him.

"Thank you, lad." Gamba pushed forward and looked through the crowd of running legs. When he saw an elephant that appeared to be the same age as Tusker, he shouted down to her. "Are you Thandi?"

She glanced up at him without losing a step. "Yes."

"Tusker wants you to keep going."

"You've seen him?" Her voice was quite anxious.

"Yes...." Gamba did not know what else to say. He was not quite sure how to describe the spectacle he had seen earlier. For all he knew, the uprights would kill him at any moment. He had no reason to believe Tusker would remain alive.

"Good. Now, we must find a way to save him." Thandi stopped in her tracks and looked up at him. "Now, tell me which direction they took him."

"Excuse me?"

"Which direction did they come from? Chances are they will head back that way," Thandi told him in her matter-of-fact voice.

"But how do you know he is alive?"

"The heart knows, good sir. Now, I can't very well chase after him. I am the matriarch of this herd, after all. So it's up to you."

"Me?" Gamba landed on the ground next to her. "How do you mean?"

"You must find the one elephant who can help him." Thandi seemed so sure of her words.

"What are you going on about?" Gamba looked at her like she had lost her mind. How in the world did she expect an elephant to go up against the uprights to rescue Tusker? "Hardly any elephant can survive against a poacher of this caliber."

"Oh, but that's where you're wrong. There is one, so magnificent Tusker's own ancestors have smiled down upon him. His name is Thunder, and his courage is well known among my kind. Find him, and tell him that a great tusker needs his assistance," Thandi charged him.

"But where will I find him?" Gamba asked her. It seemed like such a difficult task that he was not sure he should agree to it. But then again, Tusker had saved his life without thinking about the risk to his own.

"You'll find him near the beautiful lands of Gabon." Thandi watched the herd racing by her. "You must go. I have to led the others back to safety."

"Where are you going? How will we find you if we are able to break Tusker free from the uprights?"

"Hope Haven." Thandi held her trunk out to the eagle and ruffled the feathers on top of his head. "Thank you, great eagle. It is a great service you do this day."

Gamba shuddered slightly as Thandi turned and raced away from him. She had not even given him a chance to deny her request. How did she know he would not just turn around and fly the other way without looking back? Gamba looked up at the clouds that rolled in overhead. When he saw the shape of a large tusker forming high above, he knew exactly how Thandi had known. The Great Tusker was making his presence known to all of them. His anger toward the uprights who had captured his descendant was made clear as a storm brought its rage to the grounds below.

Gamba did the only thing he could do. He flew until the rains no longer pounded on his feathered wings. He would find the strength to do the right thing. He owed the gentle giant that much.

CHAPTER 5
THUNDER TAKES OFF FOR ANOTHER ADVENTURE

The dawning sun started to thread its light across the sky. Already the day was starting to fill with the sounds of waking creatures. Thunder turned to look over at his son nestled close to Kumani. Junior liked to pretend he was older than he was, but when it came down to it he was still quite a mama's boy. Thunder would not have it any other way. Innocence was not something those like him could keep for long. Thunder had kept him as safe as he could, but he knew that one day his child would experience the evils of the world. No life was ever free from worry, especially those with a price tag on their heads.

Thunder walked closer to his small herd. They were spread out across the grasses, a small herd that was growing larger by the day as new calves were

37

welcomed into its folds. Thunder was proud to be a part of it, even though he spent a lot of time away from his family fulfilling his obligation to the world around him, a task given to him from the Great Tusker in the sky. Thunder was an ambassador of good will between the uprights and the animal world. While he had come to know the world of the uprights on opposite spectrums, he believed that deep down the uprights were capable of great change. In not even an entire lifetime, Thunder had seen uprights support and protect animals that could not defend themselves, often at great risk to themselves. Thunder would never give up his quest to bring man and beast together.

Today was one of those days. He would be helping Razor take his cubs back to Sasha, before starting out on his next adventure. Thunder never knew what the road would put before him, but he did know it was time. He felt it in every bone in his body. He moved closer to his mate. "Kumani...."

"You must go again." She knew what he was about to say before he even spoke. Kumani raised her trunk to touch his.

"If I could stay forever...." Thunder felt a melancholy pass between them.

"I know, my love. The world needs you. Come

back to me in one piece. Your child will need you."

As if to demonstrate this, her belly rippled with movement. Thunder rubbed his trunk against her abdomen to soothe the growing calf beneath, and whispered to it, "I can't wait to meet you, little one."

At that moment, T.J. turned to face him. "Can I go on an adventure too?"

Thunder turned to face his child. T.J. had an impudent grin of expectation on his face. "Soon, perhaps. I'm sure your life will be filled with many adventures, Junior, but for now, you need to stay close to home."

"Aww." T.J. pouted and hung his head low. He stomped on the ground in disappointment. His movements caused the earth to shake, disrupting the sleeping caterpillar who had curled up on a rock nearby.

Katerina looked up at him through sleepy eyes. She let out a slow irritated breath as the tremors shook her whole body like a tuning fork that had been hit one too many times. The black and yellow caterpillar's anger started to grow to the point where she was like a kernel of corn ready to pop. Her cheeks took on a red tint as they puffed up in irritation. "Seriously?"

T.J. looked down at the disgruntled insect and giggled at her. He let out a small breath of air through his trunk as hysteria continued to erupt from him. The gust of air blasted the caterpillar off the rock.

When Katerina stood up on her back legs, her head was shaking in slow circles as she tried to remain conscious. Katerina started to inch away, all the while mumbling about manners and how the young elephant seemed to be lacking them. She would look for a much safer place to rest, away from such juvenile behavior.

"That wasn't very nice, T.J.," admonished Kumani.

He hung his head in shame. "Sorry."

"Your mother's right, Junior. We should respect all creatures great and small, especially if we expect them to care about our kind."

"Like you'll be here to stop me...," T.J. muttered under his breath. The young elephant did not mean to be so cruel to Katerina. The caterpillar was just in the wrong place at the wrong time. T.J. tried to calm the anger racing through him, but he was losing the battle way too easily.

"I'll be back, Junior. Don't worry." Thunder put his trunk on T.J.'s head. He knew his son was just acting up because he did not want him to go.

"Hummmph. Well, I might not be here when you do come back." Thunder stomped his foot again.

"That's enough, T.J.!" Kumani's voice brokered no argument. Instead, T.J.'s eyes filled with small tears that he was trying very hard not to shed. He inched closer to his mother and sought her comfort.

"Time to go?" Razor called across the grass. He was busy wrestling his cubs away from his ear, as they nibbled and thrashed at him in their rascally ways.

"Yes. One moment," Thunder answered him before turning back to Kumani, who seemed to be gazing far off into the open air.

"This is always the hardest part."

"We're going to take the cubs home, and then...." Thunder did not know what would happen next, really. Only that adventure called him in ways no one would ever understand. Kumani had never tried to anchor him to one place. She knew he had a purpose that others would never know.

"Save the world?" Kumani suggested in a teasing tone.

"If only." Thunder smiled at her before he turned away. He nearly avoided Zoya as she came hurtling through the grass. Raising his front leg, he smiled when she rolled under it and then darted toward T.J.

"Hey, T.J.!" Zoya launched herself at the elephant and he barely sidestepped her attack.

"Watch it!" he warned her.

"Or what?" she taunted him. Her head shook from side to side as she crossed her eyes and stuck her tongue out at him.

T.J. stomped his feet and the ground shook under her. Her head shook slightly and her eyes rolled around in their sockets. He continued to stomp until her hair stood up on end.

"Oy yey oy yey oy!" Zoya's tongue snapped back in her mouth and she started to see tiny lights flittering near her head. "The lights…they're beautiful!"

"Come with me, goofball." Naya crept closer and picked the cub up in her mouth.

"Aww! Nuts!" Zoya crossed her paws around herself as she dangled from Naya's mouth. "See you later, T.J.!"

"Bye, Zoya." T.J. could not stop the grin that flashed across his face. He may not like to see his father leave, but he was ready to get back to some peace and quiet around there.

Thunder turned to look at his herd one last time before he left them. He shuffled his feet gently on the ground and sent his message through his feet. Goodbye was always hard to say, but Thunder knew he had to go. He would think of his family often as he journeyed on his next adventure. To what, only the Great Tusker knew.

CHAPTER 6
KALI THE ADVENTURER

The group had traveled most of the morning and into the afternoon before they stopped to rest at a small water hole not far from Razor's territory. The cubs lounged around the water's edge, batting at the faces reflecting back at them.

"Take that, you!" Rafa growled at his face. He pounced toward his reflection and fell head first into the water.

Zoya laughed so hard, she fell over backwards and bumped her head on a rock. "Ouch!"

Naya watched both of the cubs and rolled her eyes. "Infants!"

"We are not! Take it back!" Zoya sat up and growled at her sister.

"Or what?" Naya's eyebrow rose in amusement.

"Or this!" Zoya launched herself at her sister and rolled on top of her. Her tiny teeth nipped at her with very little to show for it. Instead, the little nibbles ended up tickling Naya.

"Ah-ha-ha-ha! Oh! Stop! Ah-ha-ha-ha!" Naya tried to push her sister away, but by this time, Rafa had joined in. Soon, the air was filled with playful shrieks as Naya wrestled her siblings on the ground.

"Looks like the cubs know how to play dirty," Thunder chuckled.

"Learned from the best," Razor grinned.

"Sasha?" teased Thunder.

Razor huffed slightly and gave him a goofy grin. "Yeah. I'm sure she's had a long enough break. So where are we headed?"

"Into the water," Thunder answered him with a smile.

"Not now. I mean after we drop off the cubs."

"You're coming with me?" Thunder's voice was filled with surprise.

"Yes. I think it's time for the guys to hit the road." Razor was filled with a need for adventure. He had been with the cubs long enough. It was time to do something worthwhile with his life.

"I don't know, Razor. What if Sasha needs the help?" Thunder waded into the water.

"She's a fierce lioness. She barely needs me." Razor flicked a bug away from his ear.

As Thunder neared the water, the tiny stowaway creature that was hiding on the fluff of his tail started to panic. Katerina had fallen onto his tail earlier that morning, in a last-ditch effort to find a safer place to hide from the other animals. The swaying tail had rocked her to sleep for most of the day, but now that it was inches from the water, she started to panic. "Hey! Watch it!"

Thunder heard the tiny voice and turned to it. He tried to squeeze his eyes so that he could see her better, but he almost went cross-eyed. "Hello?"

"Can you set me down, please?" Katerina called up to him.

"Sure." Thunder walked closer to edge of the water and touched his tail to a large boulder.

Katerina inched off of him carefully. When she made it to the rock safely, she breathed a sigh of relief. It was short-lived however, as one of the cubs leapt into the air and made a cannonball into the water. The large splash that followed drenched every inch of her fluffy body. Her entire body shivered in reflex. "Can't a girl get a break?"

Thunder turned back toward the middle of the water and sighed as he let it soothe his weary joints. He sprayed water on his back to wash the heat from his skin. "I don't know where we're headed, Razor. It could be a long journey."

"I understand. We'll just touch in with Sasha and drop of the cubs. Maybe if we wait a little, inspiration will hit," suggested Razor.

"That's too true. That's often the way it works. Let's—" Thunder was about to say more when they were interrupted from a loud squawk from above.

"Ahhh! Watch out! Incoming!!" A flurry of pink feathers and dust fluttered through the air before it crashed into the water nearby.

"What was that?" Naya uttered in confusion.

"Not a what, but a who!" the voice answered when a black beak popped up from the surface.

"O-kay…," Naya answered. The lioness walked closer to the water and peered through its depths.

A small flamingo burst from the top and leapt onto the shore near Naya. She shook her feathers and water spurted everywhere around her. When she was done her feathers stood up on end, making her look like a pink French poodle who had been recently fluffed. Kali took her wingtips and smoothed the feathers back on her skin. She was an odd bird, wearing a long flowing white scarf and a small pilot's hat that looked like it had been made for a small child. Tilting her head curiously, the flamingo looked around her. "You must be Thunder!!!"

"Uhm...yes. But how do you know that?"

"Well, Uncle Freddie says you are always surrounded by unusual animals, like this lion here." Kali pointed to Razor, who was now standing on all fours regarding her with curiosity.

"That's Razor." Thunder smiled at the tiny flamingo. She was just as ostentatious as her uncle Frederick, but in different ways. While he was filled with flash and décor that made him stand out like a diamond in the rough, this little flamingo was just as loud and boisterous. She was on a whole different level though.

Right now, the flamingo was walking over to Razor. She put her wingtips inside his mouth and examined his teeth. Razor almost choked on his laughter, when Kali pushed his mouth all the way open and stuck her head inside it. "Wow! Great teeth! Do you have a dentist?"

Razor reached out with his paw and grabbed her around her long, thin neck. She squawked slightly before he set her safely away from him. "Do you mind?"

"No, not really. It's not a problem at all. Your breath, however, it could use some work. I have some fresh mint here." Kali pulled a leaf from behind her scarf and held it up innocently.

When Thunder saw the perplexed look cross Razor's face, he knew that his friend had met his match. Thunder laughed so hard his insides hurt when the flamingo tried to use her scarf as floss. Razor just stood there transfixed in place until Naya took pity on her father and used her head to butt the intruder away.

"Hey!" Kali held up her wings and curled her wingtips into a fist. "You want to go, furrball?"

"Who is she?" Zoya whispered to Rafa.

"I don't know, but I like her," he grinned.

"I'm Kali, the adventurer." She put her wings at her sides and took a hero's stance.

"Of course you are," muttered Naya. The lioness rolled her eyes and let out a disgusted huff.

"How is Frederick these days?" Thunder asked her.

"Oh, you know. Same 'ole, same 'ole. I spend a lot of time with him. He always says I'm going to turn him grey before his time, but I've never seen his feathers anything but a flaming shade of pink." Kali fanned the air as if mimicking her uncle's flair for the dramatic.

"What are you doing here, Kali?" Razor settled back to the ground and waited for her reply. He knew it would be interesting at the very least.

"Well, I wanted to find adventure. And Frederick always said adventure had a way of finding you. So, I went to find you." Kali made a gesture in the air as if she were connecting one dot to another. "Find Thunder. Find adventure."

Razor chuckled. "You have no idea, kid."

"Hush…," Thunder warned him. He did not like the idea of having a young flamingo along for the trip. It could be dangerous for her, if things went south. "We're taking the cubs home. You're welcome to go that far with us," offered Thunder.

"Really? Oh gee, that would be super!" Kali flashed a bright smile at them. "I can't wait to tell the others I got to go on an adventure with Thunder!"

"Oh, brother!" Naya rolled her eyes and put her paws over her head as she lowered it to the ground.

"It was bad enough that these two are here. And now this one?"

"Hey, I only add to the ad-venture. See add…it's in the word adventure. Sort of."

Naya groaned. "Ugh. When are we taking off again?"

"Soon, Naya," Razor chuckled.

"Just relax for now, Kali. Enjoy the water with us." Thunder welcomed her into the water. She crept slowly forward, and the two began a wild water fight that soon drenched the animals around them.

Katerina pulled a leaf from the tree near the rock and held it up like an umbrella over her head. The caterpillar shook her head at the craziness. "Animals!"

CHAPTER 7
CRONAN VS. NAYA

As the entourage of traveling animals approached the savanna, a pair of malicious eyes was watching from afar. The dark maned beast snarled slightly when Razor nuzzled up against the lioness who was lounging under a tree. The jealousy that ripped through Cronan made his ears steam.

"She chose that *thing?*" A loud cackle erupted near the lion, as Lyca hooted and hollered next to him. "Are you serious?"

"Shut it." Cronan's paw smashed into the painted dog's face, and Lyca whimpered like a frightened puppy.

"What he meant to say was you should be her mate," Sagara interjected. The black banded jackal knew when to push the lion's buttons. Right now was not one of those times.

"She was supposed to be mine, before the uprights entered the picture." Cronan snarled at the thought of the two legged creatures who had created much havoc in his life.

"It seems to me that you could take that one pretty easily." Sagara gestured to the lion, who was surrounded by bumbling cubs.

"Perhaps." Cronan would love to take his rightful place by Sasha's side. He watched the family reunion with a bitter taste in his mouth. As a young lioness made her way through the tall grass, his eyes nearly fell out of his head. "Wait a minute now. What is that lovely creature?"

"The flamingo?" Lyca wiped his eyes with his paws as he tried to zoom in on the animals across the clearing.

"No, you fool." Cronan gritted his teeth and let out a loud huff of air that puffed his mane back from his face. "I'm surrounded by fools."

"Hey!" Sagara snarled at him briefly, but when a loud rumble could be heard from Cronan's chest, the jackal stepped back and held a paw up. "Kidding... kidding."

"I don't know what you're talking about. I'm a

natural born wolf. I'm a fierce warrior." The painted dog sat back on his haunches and tried to howl at the moon that was invisible in the sky. His loud yammering came out much like a drowned cat as his howl caught in his throat.

"Are you going to pursue the young lioness?" Sagara asked him, but the lion was already stalking his prey. Sagara watched the lion use his stealth to move through the grass. "Females…they're nothing but trouble."

Lyca held up his paw. "Preach!"

***

As Cronan made his way across the plains, Razor picked up his scent. He turned to the cubs and pushed them closer to his mate. "Stay here."

"Where are you going, Papa?" Rafa asked him. He could sense the danger.

"Not to fear, Rafa. I'll be nearby." Razor tousled his fur before moving away.

"Where's Naya?" There was fear in Sasha's voice. They had already lost one cub to a predator. Aesop had been the weaker of their litter, making him an easy target. Razor would never forgive himself for his loss. It was the cycle of life that they all walked. Life began and it ended. Sometimes much too soon.

"Don't worry, Sasha. I will protect her," Razor assured her. "You two, stay here."

"Aww…I wanted to come." Zoya was irritated.

"Patience, little one. You'll get your turn soon enough," consoled Sasha. She started to give her cub a tongue bath and Zoya squirmed beneath her.

"Eww!"

"Oooh, do me!" Kali clapped excitedly next to them. The flamingo hopped closer and assumed a grooming position. She stood up on one leg and her other bent beneath her.

"Is she serious?" Rafa's mouth fell open.

"Sure. Why not? I like a good bath," Kali answered him.

"We should have left her at the watering hole…," Zoya whispered to Rafa.

"Right?" Rafa held up a paw to his head and made crazy little circles with it.

"Hey, I heard that!"

Thunder shook his head at their antics. He turned to Razor. "Should I come?"

"Couldn't hurt." Razor dove into the grass and disappeared.

As the pair of them traveled through the plains,

they found Naya was snarling at an approaching intruder, a lone lion who was at least double her age. Razor put his hand up to stop Thunder's movement. "You stay here. I'll go around the back."

Naya swatted at Cronan when he tried to pounce on her. "Get off me!"

The pair rolled around in the grass and Thunder felt his heart leap in his throat. Naya was a young lioness, not a cub like the others. He knew that Sasha had trained her well, but he still felt his heart racing in his chest.

Naya thrashed at the older lion. The two of them toppled over each other and a fierce wrestling match began between the two of them. Her razor sharp teeth tore into his ear, and the lion yelped beneath her. She roared fiercely at him as he bucked her off.

"You sow!" Cronan's eyes were now wild with anger. The young lioness had torn part of his ear from his head. He was prepared to take his revenge. The lion leapt through the air at her, and was pushed away at the last moment as Razor dove through the air.

"Why don't you pick on someone your own size?" Razor taunted him as the two landed in a heap.

"What? You? You must be joking." An evil laugh

poured from the cat's lips.

Razor snarled at him. "Time to go!"

Cronan lunged at Razor at the same time Thunder came barreling through the grass. Thunder stomped so hard that Cronan rolled off balance the second he landed. Seeing he had met his match for the moment, Cronan got to his feet and started to run from the clearing. He turned when he was at the edge and snarled at them. "This isn't over."

"Looks over to me!" Naya taunted him. "Unless you want to lose another ear!"

"Naya!" Razor admonished her.

"What? He'll think twice before he messes with me again. Idiot!" Naya sniffed in irritation.

"It's true. She did kick the dust out of his fur," Thunder chuckled.

"True." Razor grinned at his daughter and walked slowly toward her. "Always keep a clear head in battle."

Naya chuckled. "Like you did when you saw him attacking me?"

Razor sighed and shook his head. "You're still young, Naya. You have much to learn."

"That may be, but if I am old enough to hunt, I

am old enough to take care of myself." Naya's chin butted out defiantly.

"I don't think this is a battle you will win right now, Razor. Perhaps we should head back?" Thunder suggested.

"Good idea. Maybe Sasha can talk some sense into her." Razor ignored the roll of Naya's eyes. They traveled back to the trees where Sasha was waiting with the cubs.

Sasha looked over both of them thoroughly and neither one protested. They knew that this was Sasha's way. She was used to Razor getting into different mishaps, but this was the first time her child had faced off with another entity. "Are you all right, Naya?"

"Yes, Mom. I'm fine. He'll not forget me anytime soon." Naya had a proud smile displayed on her face.

"Good. That's the way it should be," Sasha smiled.

"You do realize she could have been killed." Razor looked at her incredulously.

"Unlikely. Besides, she needs to learn how to defend herself. It's not like there are a lot of us out there. I want her to stand strong in the face of the fight." Sasha sat up on her hind legs and held her head high. "You do know I took care of myself well before you came into my life."

Razor looked down at the ground. "Yes. Dear."

Thunder chuckled. "All's well that ends well, I always say."

Razor snorted. "When exactly do you say that?"

"It's my new thing." Thunder grinned with mischief. He knew his friend hated when his mate was right, and to have an audience to it was more than he could bear. They dropped the subject right there as they settled in for the night. They would each take turns watching out for potential threats throughout the night, just to make sure that lion did not come back.

CHAPTER 8
THE PRANK'S ON KALI

The night was pretty uneventful. When the sun rose over the horizon, the sky was painted with a golden hue. Katerina the caterpillar was pulling a blade of grass back to munch on it, but every time it got close enough to her mouth, her tiny hands released it, making the grass slap her in the face before standing straight up again. After a few more tries, she bit into the side of the grass in frustration. She sliced it in half and it started to topple over on her like a mighty oak. "Look out below!" she called.

A handful of smaller beetles scattered out of the way as the grass fell in their path. They scowled at her before continuing on their way.

"Hey, I warned you! That's right, move it along now." She let her head rise in a slight nod as if she were challenging them to defy her.

One of them turned to face her. "What are you going to do, scare us to death?"

Katerina sucked in her breath and fought to keep herself from crying. The other bugs often teased her about her looks. "Well, at least I stand out. You all look the same."

The bug shook his head at her and joined the ranks of the other bugs. They were marching to a tune that only they seemed to know. "Left foot, right foot, here we go. Right foot, left foot, hundreds to go."

Katerina scratched her head in confusion. Hundreds of steps, or hundreds of feet? There was no way any one of them had one hundred feet. She rolled her eyes and moved to finish off the blade of grass.

The cubs were rolling around playfully on the ground. As they got closer to their favorite tree, they heard a soft snuffling sound that caught their attention. "What is that?" Rafa tilted his head in confusion.

"I don't know, Rafa. Is it a monster of some kind?" Zoya sniffed the air the way her mother had taught her. "Smells weird."

"Weird? Oh, it has to be that flighty flamingo."

Rafa pointed at the pink feathered wing that hung over the branch.

"Why is she up there? Do they normally sleep in trees?" Zoya was confused.

"I thought they slept standing up."

"I have an idea." Zoya waved her brother closer to her and whispered so quietly into his ear that he barely heard her.

He giggled at her and nodded his head. Then the two of them started to gather every little pebble they could find. When they had each gathered enough for two piles, they grabbed them in their paws and started launching them at the tree.

"Watch out, Kali! It's a meteor!"

The flamingo's beak opened and closed briefly as she let out a tiny yawn. She was barely awake when more pebbles started to head her way. One of the cubs ran to the tree and tried to shake it, while the other continued to toss pebbles into the air.

"Save yourself, Kali. The meteor's going to take us all out!" Zoya called up to her in feigned distress.

"What in the world?" When a small pebble hit her from the other side, her eyes opened wide. "I knew it! I knew it! Grab your gear. The end is near!"

The flamingo scrambled so fast that she toppled from the tree, forgetting that she could fly. Her cap fell to the side of her face and she quickly readjusted it. When she got her bearings, she flapped her wings at her sides. The small scarf she wore flapped in the breeze. "Hop on! I'll carry you to safety!"

At this point Thunder glanced over at the commotion. He walked closer to the cubs. "What is she going on about, Zoya?"

Zoya gulped slightly. "Oh…nothing. She's just a birdbrain."

"Watch out, Thunder! The sky is falling!" Kali flew to his head and tried to shield him from the onslaught from above as she spread her pink wings over him.

Thunder used his trunk to reach for the frightened flamingo. He lowered her to the ground and patted her on the head. "I think we'll be all right, Kali. I'm pretty sure these two have something to tell you."

Rafa looked at his paws. He refused to look up. When Thunder stomped slightly in the dirt he jumped to attention. "Sorry, Kali. It was just a joke."

"A joke?" Kali looked as if she were about to explode for a moment, then she let out a large gust of air. "Ohh-hhooo-hooo! That's a good one! I can't believe you got me!"

Zoya's mouth dropped open in surprise. The cub had not expected the flamingo to find their prank funny. She could not help but smile at the bird. "It was my idea really."

"Oh! You're good! I could learn a thing or two from you."

Thunder smiled at the young ones. He remembered when he was a young calf. He had gotten into quite a few hijinks with his friends. "As long as you're all getting along."

Calm started to settle over them, and the children went off to find some fun while the adults still rose from their sleep. Thunder kept his eyes to the distance, for a slight prickling sensation went through him, as if a forewarning that something was headed their way. A loud screech echoed through the air as some winged creature soared overhead. Thunder tilted his head and tried to get a better view, but his eyes were no good judge from this distance.

The bird flew down to the tree next to him and peered down at him. "Are you the great Thunder?"

Naya giggled nearby. "Great? Is that what we're calling you now?"

Thunder shook his head at her. "Don't start,

Naya."

"Oh, great and wise, Sir Thunder." Naya bowed as low as she could, her voice dripping in sarcasm with each syllable.

"Don't mind her. Yes, I'm Thunder. Can I help you?" Thunder looked closer at the bird in the tree. It was an African sea eagle. His beautiful white feathers crested over his head and down his back, separating the dark brown feathers from the rest.

"I'm Gamba. And yes, you can. You must come at once! Tusker needs your help."

"Tusker?" By this point, Razor had joined in the conversation.

"Do you know him?" Thunder asked him.

"Do I know him? Are you serious? You've never heard of Tusker?" Razor shook his head at Thunder. "He's one of the last of his kind."

"He will be the last if the uprights have their way. They captured him right after he rescued me from their cages." Gamba's face was covered in guilt. "His mate, Thandi, told me to find you. You are his only hope."

Thunder looked over at Razor and knew he did not have to utter a single word to his friend. "I was waiting for a sign. Here it is. Looks like it's time to get into action."

Razor looked back at Sasha, who was grooming her paws. She stopped mid lick and smirked at him. "As if you had to ask. Just come back home to me when you're done."

"I will." Razor walked over to his mate and touched his head to hers. His dark mane ruffled in the wind.

"You're not thinking of going without me, are you?" Naya had her feet planted firmly on the ground, ready for any argument from her parents. When neither one answered her, she continued her argument. "I just proved I can take care of myself. I'm ready for adventure! I'm not a child!"

Razor and Sasha's eyes met, seeming to communicate without words. Razor nodded to Naya. "Very well. But you'll be doing most of the hunting."

Naya rolled her eyes. "I already do!"

Razor sighed. "Teenagers!"

Thunder grunted. "Ready?"

"Sure! Let me get my hat on straight." Kali stood up and twisted her hat. She licked her wingtip and held it up in the air, as if testing the wind pressure around her. "I think we should go…that way!"

"Who said she was coming?" Naya interjected.

"No one. Look kid, you should go back to your pond." Razor held his ground.

Kali crossed her wings over herself. "Bah! Like you can stop me. Can you fly?"

"No…." Razor was slightly bemused.

"Well, I can! And you can't stop me." Kali leapt into the air and flapped her wings loudly. She veered to the left and then the right, before she straightened herself and took to flight. "Which way?"

"You ready for this?" Thunder asked him with a grin plastered on his face.

"I may be bald by the time we get back, but yeah, I'm ready." Razor shook his mane out.

"Which way, Gamba?" Thunder asked Gamba.

The eagle leapt into the air. "Follow me!"

The three of them traveled on land, with Razor and Naya taking the flanks. Thunder walked as fast as he could, but he conserved as much energy as he could. This would be a long journey. The two birds flew overhead. From time to time Kali could be heard singing some silly song, as carefree as a lark.

CHAPTER 9
CRONAN'S PLOTTING REVENGE

As the entourage made their way through the savanna, dark eyes followed their every movement. Cronan had more than a beef with Razor and his offspring. He had a full blown out vendetta. His ear twitched painfully when he raised his paw up to touch it.

"You'll get what's coming to you." He held up his paw and made an angry fist with it.

"Who are you talking to, Cronan?" Lyca sidled up next to him. The painted dog tilted his whole body toward Cronan, as if that would make his eyesight less addled. He leaned over so far that he fell into Cronan.

"No one, you nitwit." Cronan pushed him away with a quick flick of his paw.

When Lyca crashed into the ground beside the lion, Sagara started to giggle. The jackal put his paws to his mouth and tried to conceal the ridiculous sound coming from his mouth. The short yips came out much like a hiccup. Before he knew it, Sagara was laughing so hard his side started to hurt. When he finally stopped laughing he turned to Cronan. "Plotting are we, Cronan? Who shall we take down first? Father or daughter?"

"Or both?" Lyca suggested. He was now watching the group of animals that was traveling without a care in the world. As he watched Thunder moving through the tall grasses, he imagined himself feasting on a large leg of meat. He shuddered in anticipation. "Can I have a wishbone?"

"What are you yammering about?" Cronan asked him.

"A wishbone…you know, that big bone that you make a wish on." Lyca's tongue lolled out of his mouth and slobber dripped down it.

"Wipe your mouth, you driveling mutt. If anyone gets to feast on elephant, it's me." Sagara used his paws to slam Lyca's mouth shut.

The painted dog yelped with his teeth slammed down on his tongue. He held his tongue in his paw as he spoke. "Dat's ut oooo ink."

Sagara scrunched one of his eyes closed as he tried to decipher the looney dog's words. After a few seconds he gave up and rolled his eyes at Lyca. Sagara moved closer to Cronan. "So what do you have planned?"

"I'm not sure yet. But when I do figure it out, I'll need all the help I can get. Summon the others." Cronan stood up and stretched his hind legs.

"The *whole* pack?" Sagara looked a little concerned.

"Yes…the *whole* pack." Cronan glared at him.

"Well, you know how out of control Lyca's family can get. Remember the last fiasco?" Sagara reminded him. The pack of wild dogs was all vicious, and all seemed to have the same mental issues that Lyca had. For some reason, the dogs thought they were natural descendants of the wolves, but this bunch of canines was not even remotely capable of their ferocity.

"They dare not refuse me." Cronan picked up a small stick from the ground and crushed it in his fist in emphasis.

Lyca gulped and a lump moved up and down his throat. He looked as if he were ready to climb up the closest tree. "I'll get them."

"Good. Don't take too long." His eyes flashed

dangerously.

"Right, boss." Lyca turned from them both with his tail slightly between his legs. He did not look forward to the family reunion he was about to have.

Sagara moved closer to Cronan. "Don't worry, Cronan. I think the new look suits you."

A warning rumble could be heard in the lion's chest as he turned to face the jackal. "Don't you have somewhere to be?"

"Yes!" His voice came out in a frightened squeak before Sagara dashed after his friend. "Wait up, Lyca!"

Cronan stared down at the animals that were traveling as if they had no care in the world. Their naiveté ate at him like acid, eroding every sane thought from his head until all he was left with was a thirst for revenge.

***

Many miles away, Tusker was waking up for the first time since he had been taken down. His eyes swam slightly as he tried to open them. He had never felt this drowsy before in his life. He tried to push himself up, but he seemed to be frozen in place. Large metal cuffs bit into his flesh as he struggled against them.

"Relax, old man," a young voice called to him.

Tusker zoomed in on the sound and saw a young female elephant standing over him. "Who are you?"

"I'm Lala. This is Pace, and Talulla." She gestured to the male and female elephant near her.

"Lala, you've got to save yourself before the uprights come back." Tusker tried to pull against the chains that bound him. He winced at the pain of metal slicing into his skin.

"Stop! You'll only make it worse." Pace, a young elephant bull warned him. His tusks had been there a year or two tops.

Talulla snickered. "They always struggle at first. It won't do you any good, I'm afraid."

"Help me out of these, will you?" Tusker asked them.

"We would if we could, but we can't." Pace gestured to his legs. "We don't have the right equipment. No opposable thumbs, you see."

"Besides, they'll be back in a few minutes. You wouldn't get far at all," Lala added.

Tusker found it odd that there were three solitary elephants just standing over him. They seemed to know quite a bit about the uprights who had captured him. How was that possible? And why were they standing there without fear of their return? Something did not add up. "Where are your chains?"

"Oh, he thinks we're prisoners. Isn't that cute?" Talulla chuckled briefly before turning away from the tortured look in Tusker's eyes.

"Look old man, we have one job. And that is to whip you into shape," Pace informed him.

"Whip me into shape for what?" Tusker was confused.

"Why, your new life, of course." Lala gave a big smile. "It will be glorious."

"Aren't they going to kill me?" Tusker asked her.

"No. Why would they do that?" Talulla stopped digging in the dirt with her tusk and turned to face him.

"It's what the uprights do." Tusker lay his head back down and sighed. "Perhaps I should just stop breathing and make it easier for them."

"No, they don't. These uprights have taken care of us ever since we were calves. We only go out with them when they need our help. This time they want us to help you to your new home." Talulla seemed convinced.

"My new home?" Tusker snorted. "Do you believe everything they tell you?"

"Yes! They are our masters. They take care of us." Talulla turned to the sound of small feet on the dirt behind her. "Oh! Here they come. Look alive, everyone."

A group of uprights approached them. They came closer to Tusker and started to jerk on his chains. At first Tusker fought their intrusion, but the elephants egged him on.

"Get up, you fool! Don't make them use their lightning rods!" Pace warned him.

"What's a lightning rod?" Tusker did not like the sound of it, whatever it was.

"It's a stick filled with lightning. If you don't get up, they'll shock you with it." Lala looked as if she had met the rod head-on at some point.

Tusker could not believe any animal who had been subjected to such cruelty would actively assist the uprights that hurt them. As much as he was ready to move to the next lifetime, he did not want to go out in that fashion. He used his inner strength to rise from the ground.

"That's it!" cheered Talulla.

"Great. Now, let's get a move on, old man." Lala

nodded to the west.

"My name is Tusker, and while I may be old, I prefer you use my name," he grumbled at them.

"Whatever you say, Tusker. Just keep moving and you will be fine," Lala ordered him.

Tusker did not think he was going to be fine at all. These uprights were not to be trusted, but for now he did not seem to have a way out. His heart was heavy as he thought of his beloved Thandi who he had left behind. Had she made it out all right? Maybe there was still hope that he might see her again in this lifetime. As long as there was hope, Tusker had to push on.

CHAPTER 10
MORE FRIENDS ON THE HORIZON

The group had already traveled for a few days through the grasslands and into the forest, and had decided to stop for the day to replenish their energy. They could not keep up this mad pace if they were going to be any help to Tusker.

Thunder was lost in thought as he started to dig for some food. He had no idea that a tiny caterpillar was nestled safely on his tusk. Katerina had used tiny silky strands to keep herself attached safely on the end of his tusk. When he started to move toward the ground, the caterpillar's eyes grew large. She quickly used her teeth to break free from the strands. As Thunder's left tusk started to dig into the ground, Katerina was catapulted into the air. She landed in a small heap on the ground and was a trembling mess.

Katerina's back hunched down slightly in defeat. "Why do I even bother? I'll never be a butterfly."

"Aww! You're adorable!"

Katerina found herself face to beak with Kali. The flamingo beak was so large, Katerina thought she would soon be food. The caterpillar shrieked and fainted before her.

"Hmmm…what do you think her problem is?" Kali used her wings to fan the tiny caterpillar. When that did not work to revive her, she started to push on her abdomen, and the air came out of Katerina's mouth in tiny squeaks.

When Katerina's eyes opened, she looked up at the flamingo and feared for her life. "Please don't eat me!"

"Eat you? Why would I eat you? I only eat leaves." Kali rolled her eyes comically.

Naya, who was listening from nearby, was wrinkling her nose in amusement. "That explains so much."

Katerina smiled at Kali. "I eat leaves too."

"Smashing! We'll get along just fine then. Here." Kali handed a small leaf to the caterpillar, who began to wolf it down like it was nothing. "You're sure a voracious eater!"

"I'm just big boned." Katerina crossed her now chubby arms around her middle. The caterpillar had been stockpiling enough food to feed her for days. She just could not get enough. She sniffed at Kali and started to inch away.

"I didn't mean anything by it! Wait, come back...." Kali called as if she were a far distance away from her, but the caterpillar was about as fast as a snail crawling up a rock.

Naya rolled her eyes at the two of them and went to see what her father was up to. She found him lurking under a tree. "What are you doing, Father?"

Razor looked over at his daughter and gave her a forced smile. "Taking in the view."

"You're lying," Naya accused him.

"Why would I lie to you, Naya?" Razor turned back to the horizon.

"What's out there?"

"I'm not sure. But I don't like it." Razor's hair stood on end slightly as his nerves got the best of him.

"Is it that lion?" Naya knew she hit the nail on the head with that as a loud rumble started to form in her father's belly. "Don't worry about him, Dad. We can take him."

"What do you mean we? You nearly had him all by yourself." Razor held his paw up and the two of them bumped paws together.

"You know it! Hey, there's a carcass just down the hill there. We could see if there's anything left on it," suggested Naya. Her tummy growled in hunger.

"Why don't you get a head start?" Razor suggested. He watched as Naya zipped away before he could say another word. Standing up, he stretched slightly, then walked to where Thunder was foraging.

"Are they following us?" Thunder asked him.

"How did you know?" Razor was stumped.

"Because you're a dad and it's what we do. We always look out for potential threats to our offspring. Second only to their mothers, of course." Thunder smiled at him.

"I haven't seen them for a while, but they were following us closer to home. They have either given up or they're regrouping." Razor swiped his claws into the dirt to help free the root Thunder was digging for.

"Thanks!" Thunder plopped it into his mouth and started to half-chew, half-speak. "Does she know why you let her come?"

"No. Not really. She thinks I am giving her a taste

of adventure. If she knew I was just trying to keep her safe from that lunatic, she wouldn't take it so well. Teenagers!" Razor rolled his eyes in exasperation.

"Someday she'll have cubs of her own and understand." Thunder wiped the crumbs from his mouth with his trunk and looked around for more food.

Gamba joined them from above. The eagle had been scouting ahead of them. He was a remarkable lookout. "I've news."

"Oh?" Thunder's eyebrows rose in surprise. "Is it the tusker?"

"No...but they seemed to know you." Gamba scratched his claws on the tree bark next to him as he considered his next words. "A ragtag group of fellows if you ask me."

Razor snorted. "He seems to collect them."

"I do not...." Thunder looked around him, as if that would help his argument. He saw the young flamingo looking under every rock...for what, the world might never know. "Okay, you may have a point there. What do they look like?"

"Hmmm...well, two of them are rather fluffy looking, two gorillas that were yammering about some cowboy days."

"Ah. Yeah. That would be Harold and Neville. They've watched one too many upright movies at Hope Haven, I'd guess. I don't know why they insist on sneaking in when the uprights are out."

"True. I never did understand the fascination of the tiny glass box they stare at," agreed Thunder.

"That's just because you can't see that well," Razor pointed out.

"I do well enough." Thunder let out an irritated huff of air.

"Well, that's all fine and dandy. Any idea why they would bring a rhinoceros with them? With three egrets to boot?" Gamba was clearly confused.

"I can see where you might question that. If I had a guess, I would say the gorillas have found one of our friends. Salem," Thunder answered. It had been a long time since they had last seen the rhino. Thunder hoped that everything was all right with him.

"How far away are they, Gamba?" Razor looked up at the eagle.

"Well, if we left now we would reach them in a few hours. They're traveling this direction. Shall we go?"

Thunder seemed to be debating his next words. "Sure. Why not? It couldn't hurt to have more friends to help us along the way. Who knows what we'll be up against when we find Tusker? Which way, Gamba?"

"Follow me!" Gamba leapt into the air and flapped his wings with ease.

"I'll just go get Naya. We'll be right behind you."

Thunder turned to Kali, who was speaking into a hole in the ground. He called out to her. "Coming, Kali?"

The flamingo turned to face him and a bright smile seemed to light up her beak. "You betcha!"

At first, Kali did not look where she was headed and bumped smack dab into a tree. She shook her head slightly as she tried to still the swirling lights around her. "Oops. I seem to have run aground."

"Why don't you ride on my back for a bit, Kali?" suggested Thunder. He did not have the time to worry about her lack of any real flight pattern. He started to wonder who had given her flying lessons. Surely, not Frederick. He was a pretty seasoned flyer.

"Thank you!" Kali soared down to Thunder's back and wrapped her wings lovingly around him.

Thunder hated to admit it. Even though she was a pain in the rear, he was started to become pretty fond of the little pink bird, eccentricities and all. He chuckled slightly as he thought about how opposite she was from Frederick, yet equally harebrained at the same time. He continued to follow the bird that soared above them, hoping to run into the gorillas before nightfall.

CHAPTER 11
JABARI DROPS FROM THE TREES

The edge of the forest zipped by them as they raced after Gamba out into the grasslands of the savanna. It had been quite some time since Thunder had seen his friends. He wondered what adventures the zany gorillas had gotten into since the last time he had seen them. Were they wrangling other animals like the cowboys they wanted to be?

Gamba flew down to the nearest tree and called down to him. "They're right on the horizon there. Do you see them?"

Razor chuckled. "With those eyes?"

"I may not be able to see them yet, but I can hear them." Thunder stood still and let his feet read the vibrations that were being sent through the ground. "Sounds like they're heading this way."

"Good. I'm staying right here then." Naya plopped down on the ground. She was not prepared to move another step. While she was a pretty active lioness, the adventure was already taking its toll on her. The teen was getting snippier by the moment.

"Oh come on! We got this!" Kali charged off of Thunder's back with her wings flapping wildly about her.

"Easy for you to say! You've gotten a free ride the whole time." Naya rolled her eyes at the flighty flamingo.

"You think guiding him in the right direction is easy?" Kali sniffed at her. "If it weren't for me, we'd be lost."

Four pairs of eyes zoomed in on the flamingo as if she had completely lost her mind. Gamba was the first to say a word. "If you're so helpful, where are the gorillas?"

"In the mist...duh!" Kali's head rotated in exaggerated circles.

"What in the world are you going on about?" Naya's eyebrow arched and a look of disdain was etched on her face. She moved a little further away from the bird. "I think I'm going to stay over here."

"Why?" Kali flapped her wings some more and

soared lightly through the air. She settled in the tree next to Gamba, staring down at Naya with curious eyes.

"I don't want to catch what you got."

"Oh no!" Kali started so rifle through her feathers as if she were searching for some hidden disease. She lifted up her pilot's hat and closed one eye as she peered inside it before plopping it back down on her head. "What do I have?"

"Bird brain!" Naya let out a disgusted huff of air.

"Hey!" Gamba crossed his wings in front of him.

"Hey! I resemble that!" Kali stuck her tongue out at Naya and put her wing tips at the sides of her face as she shook her head.

Gamba turned to peer at her with dubious eyes. "Don't you mean you resent that?"

Kali stopped shaking her head with her tongue lolling out of her mouth. "Wait? What? Why would I resent that? I am a bird, after all. I have a brain. What's so wrong with being a bird brain?"

Gamba slapped his feathers against his face. "Oh, brother!"

A giggling sound came from the tree next to them. None of them recognized the sound. Then the laughs came so hard, the owner jumped down from the tree and landed on his backside. The boy was still laughing as he rolled on the ground.

A collective gasp came from the group of animals. They edged away from the upright boy, and were prepared to run at the first sign of danger. Thunder was the only one who looked at him for the innocent boy he was. He had far more experience with uprights, from those that wanted to hurt to those that wanted to help.

"Don't be afraid. He's just a boy," Thunder told them.

Jabari stood up and brushed himself off. He was wearing a red and white striped shirt with green cargo pants. He put his hands on his hips and his chin jutted out in slight defiance. "I'll have you know I'm ten! I'm hardly a baby."

Thunder blinked in confusion. Was the boy talking to him? He regarded him cautiously.

Razor stepped closer to Thunder and whispered to him. "Thunder, did he just talk to you?"

"You're Thunder?" An excited look flashed across his face. "I've always wanted to meet you. I've heard so much about you."

"And you called me bird brained!" Kali snorted.

"They think they can talk to an upright! Ah-ha-ha-ha!"

Jabari smirked slightly. He looked up at the flamingo and waved. "Nice hat! Where did you get it?"

Kali's beak fell open in shock and she nearly fell out of the tree. If Gamba had not held his wings out to steady her, she would have toppled over. She rubbed her eyes and tried to refocus them. Turning to Gamba, she put a wing on him. "Pinch me! I have to be dreaming. Even I couldn't think this up!"

"I'll do it!" Naya had a wicked gleam in her eye.

Thunder stepped closer to the boy and really looked at him. For some reason, he was reminded of a young girl he had met a long time ago. He smiled at the boy and extended his trunk. "I'm Thunder."

"I'm Jabari!" The young African boy walked closer, and instead of touching his trunk, Jabari hugged it like he had met a long lost friend. "My mom's not going to believe this!"

"I could see how this would be hard to believe. The whole talking to animals thing is unbelievable," Razor chuckled. "How long have you been talking to animals?"

"For as long as I can remember." Jabari stepped

away from Thunder and walked closer to Razor. When he saw the lion step back slightly, he held a hand up. "Not to worry, friend. I was just checking for your scar. You've healed up nice."

"How do you know I have a scar?" Razor's mane ruffled slightly in the breeze.

"My mom. She told me all about it. There's only one lion who would run around with Thunder. We never knew why though."

Thunder could not contain his curiosity any longer. "And who exactly is your mother?"

"Imani, of course!" Jabari shook his head as if he thought Thunder should have known the answer to that question.

Thunder smiled. Now he knew why the face looked so familiar. Imani was the girl they had saved from drowning. She had grown up into a fierce advocate for the animals around her. "What are you doing here, Jabari?"

"I was looking for Tusker," he answered him matter-of-factly.

"Tusker?" Razor stepped closer. "How does he know about Tusker?"

"Who doesn't know about Tusker? My people have spoken of him for quite some time." Jabari sat down on the ground and crossed his legs under him. "I was minding my own business when I heard some birds talking about his capture. So I did the only thing I could do. I set out to free him."

"And where are the rest of the uprights?" Razor sniffed slightly.

"What do you mean?" Jabari asked them.

"What Razor means is you're just a boy. How are you going to set him free?"

"With a little help from my friends." Jabari gestured to the animals around him.

"It's not that easy…." Thunder did not like the idea of Imani's child putting himself in danger. If his own offspring set off like that he would be beside himself.

"Of course it is. They won't be expecting it at all. I know these poachers. They are over confident and think no one will stop them. Well, I have something to tell them. I won't stop until I do."

"Where's Imani?"

Jabari refused to meet his eyes. "She's at home."

"Then that is where we shall take you." Thunder knew that they had a job to do, but he would not let this boy come to harm. His gifts were too important.

"You can't make me!" Jabari made tiny fists that he slammed into his knees in defiance. "I have a job to do too!"

Naya stood up and walked over to Jabari. She sat next to him and put her head in his lap. "I'll protect him."

Razor and Thunder both looked at her incredulously. Naya never took to any creature, great or small. For her to give her favor toward this upright made both of them take pause. Razor was the first to respond. "Fine. But you're on kid duty."

Two pairs of eyes glared at Razor at the same time. The lion burst into laughter and shook his mane. "We've got our hands full with these two."

"Fine. But it's time to go. We've got a few friends to catch up with." Thunder nodded for the rest of the group to follow him. Once they caught up with the others, he would try to figure out what the next step was.

CHAPTER 12
HAROLD AND NEVILLE

Thunder was impressed with how well the boy kept up with them as they raced through the grass. He wondered how often the boy was off on his own. Surely, uprights did not let their children roam so freely. He had certainly never seen one this far from the others. Thunder imagined there must be something that Jabari was not telling them.

When they caught up to the storm of dust racing their way, they barely avoided a collision. Thunder held out his trunk to keep Jabari safe from the others. He knew that Jabari would be safe, it was just his need to protect him. "Whoa there!"

"Well, look here, Neville." Harold gestured to Jabari.

"Oh, it's that boy again. I swear he's been

99

following us around for quite some time, Harold." Neville glanced at Jabari.

"If I was following you around, how could I have passed you?" Jabari asked him.

Harold scratched his head in confusion. "Well, I'll be. You're right, Harold. The boy can talk."

"Of course I can talk!" Jabari snickered.

"Well, isn't that something." Neville turned to Thunder. "Did you know he could talk?"

"I got the memo," Thunder chuckled. "Where's Salem?"

"He's right behind us. Had to collect the birds first," Harold explained.

"Birds?" Thunder wondered which birds he was talking about. He did not have long to wait to find out.

Salem came charging toward them with three white egrets perched on his back, having the ride of a lifetime. They hooted and hollered as the dust settled around them. The rhino coughed slightly as the clouds rose in the air. "Ugh-huh-ugh."

"Well, hello there!" Kali flew over to the rhino's back and stuck her wing out to the first egret she could reach.

Idi looked the flamingo over curiously before he took her wing tip in his. "Hello?"

"I'm Kali. Uncle Freddie's going to flip when he finds out I met the king!"

"King? Whatever are you going on about?" The egret looked back at his siblings with a slight expression of fear on his face.

"Well, only the king could ride such a fine steed. Are these your men?" Kali waved to the other two egrets.

Awiti crossed her wings over herself. "I'm a girl!"

"Oh, well, you sure don't look like one...." Kali gestured to her scarf. "Maybe you need a scarf like mine."

Awiti started to step toward Kali with a fierce scowl on her face. She was about to pummel her, but her brothers held her back. "Let me go! I'm going to set her straight."

Kali stepped back cautiously. "I'm sorry...did I say something wrong?"

"Wrong? Oh, just let me at her."

Naya was rolling on the ground at this point. "Oh...that's just...ah-ha-ha."

Salem gestured to the flamingo on his back. "I see

why you keep this one around."

"Well, she does liven up the place," Thunder chuckled. "Kali, perhaps you should come down for a bit."

"If you say so. I just wanted to meet the king." Kali pouted as she flew over to Thunder's back.

"Look, that one there is not a king. He's my brother, and there's not a royal bone in his body." Awiti gestured to the egret to her left.

Idi scowled at his sister. "Hey, if she wants to think I'm the king, I don't see the need to correct her."

"I take that back. He is a royal pain in the —"

"Awiti!" Lumo interrupted her.

Awiti rolled her eyes at Lumo. "Just because you hatched first doesn't mean you're the boss."

"Wow…I can see why it took you longer to get here." Razor grinned at Salem. "Makes me glad my cubs are back home." Naya cleared her throat and Razor looked over at her. "Oh, right. Except for this one."

"I'm not a cub! Gah!" Naya launched herself at Razor as if to tackle him, but he ducked at the last second and she went flying through the air. She tucked into a ball and rolled safely back to her feet.

"You have to be faster, Naya," he reminded her.

Naya scratched the ground with her claws. "You won't see me coming next time."

Jabari walked over to Naya and wrapped his arms around her neck. "I believe in you, Naya."

Hearing the boy speak made the egrets stop their squabbling. They did a double take, looking from each other a few times back to the boy, who was oblivious to their stares. Salem was the first to speak. "You must be the boy who speaks."

"The boy who speaks?" Thunder asked him.

"There was a legend among our kind...surely you have heard of it? A long time ago, there was a child who could speak to the animals. He knew their hearts and they knew his. He used his gift to spread peace to the world around him."

Jabari stood up. "What happened to him?"

"He died standing up for what he believed in, I suppose." Salem looked away from Jabari and up to the sky.

Thunder could tell that Salem was not sharing the full story, but the boy did not seem to notice. Perhaps he should bring it up later when the boy was not in listening range. Thunder was afraid that the end that Salem spoke of was not something Jabari should take lightly. Instead, he changed the topic.

"Where are you headed to?" Salem asked them.

"Tusker was taken," Jabari answered as if the rhino had spoken directly to him.

Harold snorted in disgust. "Why do they always have to take the beauty from our world?"

"I wish I knew," Jabari answered him. There was sadness pooling in his dark brown eyes. His mother had clearly taught him a reverence for the animals around him.

"Well, what are we waiting for?" Awiti spoke first. "Let's go save him."

"If he's alive…," Idi interrupted her.

"Why do you gotta be like that?" Awiti shook her head at her brother.

"What, a realist? There's no way they're carting a giant elephant half-way across the savanna when all they want is…." Idi stopped talking and looked over at Thunder's ivory tusks. "Uhm…never mind."

Thunder shook his head. "I know I have a price on my head. It grows higher each day as the supply is diminished, but I will not let that keep me following the will of the Great Tusker."

Jabari stepped over and patted his hand on

Thunder's side. "My mom always told me how brave you were. I would be proud to help the great Thunder bring Tusker home safely."

Thunder bowed down lower to the ground and held his front leg out for Jabari to climb. "Hop on. We've got a long way to go."

Jabari wasted no time. He climbed up onto Thunder's back, and when he was up on top, he leaned over and scratched behind Thunder's ear. "Thank you, my friend."

"You all coming?" Thunder waited for a collective reply. When he was sure everyone around him was in, he turned to Gamba. "Lead on, Gamba!"

The small group was now more like an entourage as they made their way across the savanna. They traveled as far as they could before night fell around them. A hush fell over the world around them, and a false sense of peace blanketed them.

CHAPTER 13
TUSKER'S RESCUE

Over the next few days the group traveled as far as their legs and wings could carry them. Thunder had sent Gamba out that morning to scout the area. He was hoping that the bird would return with news that was helpful. Thunder looked up to the sky and saw the clouds forming a shape in the sky. The white puffy image was barely discernable, but Thunder knew its message.

"The Great Tusker…," he whispered. No one around him heard him, which suited him just fine. He did not want to raise their hope. They were all pushing themselves faster than they should. Thunder had a feeling that Gamba would bring news back very soon.

Thunder turned to find Jabari laying his head on

107

top of Naya. The pair were fast friends. It was good to see two creatures with such wildness come together. While Jabari was an upright, he had the heart of the fiercest cub, something he was sure Imani had ingrained in him. Thunder had no doubt that Jabari would protect them all with his life. It was his job to make sure the child never put himself in the line of fire.

"Is that Gamba squawking?" Kali asked in wonder. The flamingo rolled her wingtips together and put them up to her eyes like makeshift binoculars.

The eagle swooped down and landed so fast that his feet barely touched the ground. "It's Tusker!"

Thunder felt a slight panic enter his heart. "Is he alive?"

Gamba sucked in a huge gasp of air. "Yes... alive...with three elephants."

"Three elephants? What about uprights?" Razor asked him.

"They were nearby. He had shackles on his legs, but he was moving."

"Why would he just give in?" Naya wondered.

"Because they are using the elephants against him," Jabari answered. The animals turned to look at him as if he had grown another nose on his face.

Jabari held up a hand. "From what I heard, Cayman is one of the highest paid poachers. He uses his elephants to trick other animals."

"Why would they do that?" Thunder was very concerned. If an upright had the ability to make the animals give up and walk right into their traps, how could Thunder help keep them safe?

Jabari scratched his head. "They don't know better?"

"Oh...they know better. How could they not know better?" Naya shook her head and pointed over at Kali, who was trying to hide her head in a hole in the ground. "Even she knows better!"

"Are you sure about that?" Awiti put a wing on the rock next to her and shook her head as she sadly clucked her tongue to the roof of her beak.

"Okay, maybe not the best example, but still." Naya sat back on her haunches and her eyes peered off to the horizon. Something had caught her attention, but she was not quite sure what it was.

"So what do we do now?" Salem was the first to break the silence that had started to form around them as each of them considered their options.

"We break Tusker free from his chains." Harold stood on all four haunches.

"Right, dear boy. I second that." Neville waved his hand at the animals around him. "I'm sure we have enough brains and brawn to get him free."

Jabari grabbed a stick and sat down on the ground. He started sketching out something only he could see. After a few moments, he turned around with a big smile on his face. He pointed to his sketch in the dirt. "Okay. I got it. So…first…Thunder and Salem will distract the uprights away from where they are keeping Tusker. They will more than likely leave Tusker chained near the other elephants."

"Why would they chase those two?" Kali asked innocently.

"Let's just say we have something they want," Thunder answered the flamingo. His voice was almost cryptic.

"That's a dangerous plan, Thunder." Razor did not seem happy with the plan at all. "What if they catch you?"

"They won't." Thunder was finding it difficult to convince the others.

"We're in this together, old boy," Harold interrupted. "Besides, those uprights want all of us. Maybe we should do this instead." The gorilla started scratching out Jabari's initial plan. He drew more pictures in the line of fire.

Neville scratched his chin with one of his fingers as he read the drawings below. "I believe you're right there, Harold."

"Almost like Marco Polo," interjected Naya.

"Who's that?" Kali was peering down at the drawings.

Naya put a paw on her head as she shook it back and forth. "Nevermind, Kali."

"So, what you're saying is those on foot distract the uprights. What about the birds? You've left us out," Idi pointed out.

"How's your aim?" A smile spread across Jabari's face.

"I've hit a target here and there." Lumo whistled slightly and made an innocent face.

Awiti rubbed the back of her head. "I thought you said that was an accident?"

Idi shook his head. "Focus please! Save it for the uprights."

"Right. Keep it together, everyone. It's going to take all of us to pull this off. Who's with me?" Thunder looked around at the faces surrounding him. He hated asking for their help. This was a mission that was filled with peril, but Tusker was one of the last of his kind. Thunder was tired of losing great animals everywhere he turned.

"And me? What will my job be?" Jabari refused to be left out.

"You undo his shackles."

"I'll protect him," Naya stepped closer to him.

"You're very brave, daughter." Razor was filled with pride.

"I learned from the best." Naya nodded first to Razor and then to Thunder.

"Looks like you're doing something right, Razor." Thunder winked at him.

"Okay. Let's get over the ridge there and we'll begin." Gamba rose into the air and the birds followed him.

The animals crept as close as they could to their positions. They could see the great tusker elephant grazing next to three other elephants. He was the only one wearing chains. There were a handful of uprights around them, but only two carried guns.

Thunder looked over at Razor and gave him his cue. The lion roared his fiercest roar on the other side of the clearing. Small birds rose up from the grasses in reflex.

"What was that?" The upright named Berko stood up and brought his gun up to his shoulder, as if looking through the sight on the end would help him see further into the distance.

Thunder smirked. Uprights were so easy to read sometimes. He gave a loud trumpet from his trunk, and the other upright sat up.

Cayman gripped his gun with his right hand. He turned to the other uprights. "You three go that way. The rest of you with me. Lala, Pace, Talulla…stay."

The elephants moved closer together the moment he uttered his command. Thunder could not believe the amount of control he had over them. No upright should ever command beasts against their nature. The sadness of it all almost outweighed the anger that boiled inside him. Thunder trumpeted again and started to race away from the area.

The chase was on. As Razor, Thunder, and Salem distracted the uprights, the birds started to drop everything they could carry on top of them. Two of the uprights were hit so hard, they fell unconscious to the ground.

As two of them got closer to Thunder, the gorillas pulled the root of a tree up high enough to trip them.

The uprights fell forward and scrambled to get back to their feet. When they saw the gorilla's pounding on their chests their eyes widened in fear. They ran the other direction and almost knocked Cayman over in the process.

"What is wrong with you fools?" He pulled one of them off the ground by the scruff of his shirt.

"G...g...g...gorillas!" He yanked his shirt away from Cayman and continued to run. "You're on your own, Cayman!"

"Gorillas? Please! What use are they? We've got guns, you fools!" Cayman shook his head at the fleeing man.

"No, you have a gun and you're not paying us enough for this!" The other man followed after the first.

To the east, Razor was giving the other uprights a run for their money. His ability to crouch low in the grasses gave him quite the advantage. He came up behind them, so close his breath was on the back of the upright's neck. The upright turned around and his face went purple before he passed out in fear.

"Do you always have that effect on people?" Idi called down to him.

"Pretty much." Razor grinned up at him. "Keep it

coming up there."

While the uprights were being distracted, Jabari approached Tusker. He held up his hand at the gentle giant. "I'm here to help."

Tusker snuffed gently. "I doubt that. You're just like the others."

"I'm not like the others. If you just let me get these shackles off of you." Jabari pointed down to his legs.

Tusker tilted his head and took in the child before him. "Did you just talk to me?"

"Yes. And you talked to me. I'm Jabari, and you must be Tusker. I've heard a lot about you." Jabari crept a little closer and reached down to unbuckle the chain before Tusker could object.

"Who told you?" Tusker asked him.

"There's an eagle named Gamba who speaks quiet highly of you. He said you saved him. He went to warn Thandi, and she told him to find Thunder. Which he has." Jabari made quick work on the other shackles, which were impossible for those without opposable thumbs to remove.

Tusker was clearly impressed. "You sure get around, for a boy."

Jabari chuckled. "You have no idea."

The other three elephants were now starting to kick up their feet near him. Lala was filled with panic. "You can't go. If you do, he'll be very angry."

"Come with us," suggested Tusker.

"We can't...." Pace shook his head at the thought. "Master would find us, and he would use his lightning sticks on us."

"Suit yourself, but we don't have time to waste. You have to go, Tusker." Jabari pointed to the hills. "We'll meet the others there."

"Won't the other elephants just tell him where we're going?" Naya pointed out.

"We have to trust that they won't." Tusker started to move as fast as his legs could carry him. Naya and Jabari ran at his side, for the gentle giant could not run as fast as a younger bull could.

***

When the upright in charge realized that his team had started to disintegrate, he gave up his chase on the other animals. He returned to where the other elephants were still waiting for him. He noticed the way they trembled in fear, but that did not ease the anger boiling inside him. "You let him go!"

The three elephants gathered as close as they could as they waited for the punishment they knew was coming. Talulla wrapped her trunk around Pace and tried to shelter him from whatever came next. The hit never came.

Cayman sat down on the ground and wiped sweat from his face. This could not be the end. His pay day was still out there. He just had to regroup. When Berko came back to the clearing, Cayman stood up. "Where are the others?"

"Spooked." Berko would not meet his eyes.

"We need to regroup." Cayman turned to the elephants. "Which way did they go?"

Talulla glanced at the others. When Pace was about to move to the direction of the hills, she moved in front of him. She put her trunk on his head and turned back to Cayman. Then the elephant led him in the opposite direction. Even though she knew he would be boiling later, she knew it would buy the others some time.

CHAPTER 14
CHEER UP TUSKER

The scenery blurred past them as they all raced up the hill. When they made it to the top, they stopped only long enough to take a breath and make a quick introduction before they continued on. They could not afford to let the poachers gain on them. Thunder could tell that Tusker's mind was not quite in it, as his thoughts seemed to distract him.

"You seem deep in thought, Tusker." Thunder looked over at him. "What's wrong?"

"Those other elephants...." Tusker's voice was gruff with emotion.

"They chose not to come." Jabari was sitting on Thunder's back. He looked down at Tusker with sympathy.

"We should have pushed them harder." Tusker

closed his eyes for a moment, then looked up to the sky. "What kind of descendant am I, if I can't even convince them to run for their own freedom?"

"I think you're too hard on yourself, Tusker." If anyone understood the pressure of what others believed, he did. Ever since he was born, Thunder had a prophecy on his shoulders. He was supposed to be the bridge between man and beast. He had risen to the challenge in most instances, but he had come to realize that he could not fix everything. Sometimes there were obstacles even Thunder could not break through. Greed was the biggest one. Uprights were not the only beings in this world that let greed and rivalry rule their hearts.

The gorillas took the lead and stopped several steps ahead of the group. They picked up a few rocks from the ground and started to juggle them. One of them knocked Kali down from the sky.

"May day! May day!" Kali fell right into Neville's hands. The gorilla did not realize she was not the rock he was juggling and continued to toss her into the air. "Wheeee!"

When he realized his mistake, Neville stopped juggling and the rocks landed on top of Harold, one right after the other.

"Ouch!" Harold rubbed his head and hot air snorted out of his nose. Before Neville could stop him, Harold started chasing after him. The ruckus was so great that the ground started to shake.

Kali stood on the ground and shook her head at the chaos. "And you all call me strange."

They all seemed to pick up on the moment. They were trying to cheer Tusker up with the laughter and livelihood around them. He seemed to be oblivious to it all.

Jabari took a chance. He climbed up into the tree in front of Tusker, as high up as he possibly could. The group below was watching his every step, but Tusker still seemed oblivious. Jabari edged out onto the limb and held his arms up like a bird. "Catch me!?"

Tusker continued to walk without glancing up. Salem's eyes opened wide as he saw the boy hurtling to the ground. He raced over at the last minute and caught Jabari safely on his back. He turned back and looked up at him. "You're either crazy or out of your mind."

"Isn't that the same thing?" Idi pointed out from the air above them.

"Guys, this isn't working. Maybe we should just

focus on the journey." Thunder knew his friends meant well, but Tusker was not used to their humor. In fact, it seemed to have the opposite effect on the gentle giant. The further they traveled, the more tired Tusker appeared.

"Maybe you need a break?" Razor suggested.

Tusker looked just over the rise and a light entered his eyes. "I think you're right. I do need to rest."

"All right, let's stop right here then." Thunder started to turn around to tell the others.

"No…we're going there." Tusker pointed ahead of them. "We'll stop there."

The group traveled for a little longer and stopped just outside a path that led down to a pit of some kind. "What is this place?" Thunder asked.

"Never mind that." Tusker waved his words away easily with his own. "Why don't you look for some food?"

"Sounds like a plan. Harold and I will look for fruits. You got the vegetables, Thunder?" Neville called up to the elephant.

"On it."

"We'll get the meat." Razor grinned at them. The others made a face, since the only two meat-eaters there were the lions.

Jabari turned to Thunder. "Can I come with you?"

"Of course." Thunder liked having Jabari with them. He reminded him a lot of his own child, even though he did not have the four legs and trunk that he did. Jabari made him miss his son a little more each day. Thunder hoped he was minding his p's and q's back home, safe with Kumani. Junior would be a handful if he did not let him explore with him soon though. He was wired much like Naya, who would not have given Razor a moment's peace had he not let her come along.

"And what about us birds?" Idi asked.

"Make sure Kali doesn't injure herself." Thunder nodded to the flamingo who was so overtired, she was moving across the ground in an almost sleep walk.

"Are you sure about that?" Awiti grimaced when Lumo hit her. "I was just kidding."

"We're on it, Thunder!" Idi held his wing up to salute Thunder.

As Thunder moved through the trees around him, all he could think about was how sad Tusker had been. If his spirits did not pick up soon, the journey would only be that much harder for him to finish. They still had quite a ways to go to get to Hope Haven. It was the only place that Thunder trusted to protect a tusker like him. There were so few of them left.

***

Not far from their group, Cronan stood surveying the area. He had never seen an elephant like that before. "Is that a tusker?"

Lyca tilted his head and his tongue lolled out of his head. "What's a tusker?"

"An elephant with giant tusks." Sagara shook his head in disgust. "Don't you know anything?"

Lyca growled at him, and a large pack of wild dogs joined in as they bared their teeth in his defense. He lifted his paw and pointed to the dogs behind him. "I know these guys have my back."

"Relax, save it for them," Cronan ordered him.

Lyca stopped growling and the minions behind him relaxed. "So what's the plan, boss?"

"From what I can see here, they have to pass through that small valley there. If we wait for them on the other side, we can use the element of surprise."

"That's if they don't smell Sagara first." Lyca laughed and slapped his sides with his paw.

Sagara's top lip started to rise into a snarl, but the minute any sound left his lips, the pack started to growl at him again. "Call them off already, will you? We're on the same side, after all."

"I know, but this is soooooo much fun." Lyca grinned at him. "Never mess with a wolf pack."

"Wolf? Oh, that's just...." Sagara laughed at the thought of the painted dog ever being remotely close to a wolf.

"Silence!" roared Cronan. "Keep it together! We have a job to do."

Lyca turned to him with a confused look on his face. "What are we doing again?"

"Taking out as many as we can. Especially those fur balls that think they got the best of me."

Sagara looked up at his injured ear and held up a paw as if he were going to mention they had taken a piece of him, but he changed his mind at the last minute. "Bu...brilliant plan!"

"We move."

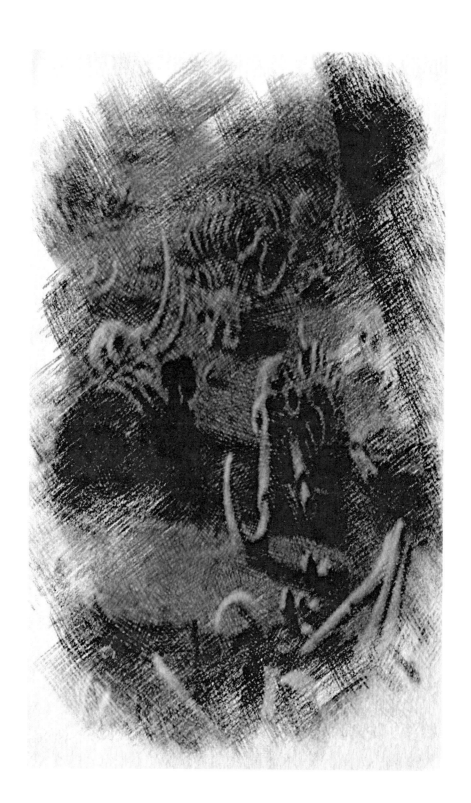

CHAPTER 15
VALLEY OF THE BONES

While the others went in search of food, Tusker continued forward into the hazy fog that seemed to surround the base of the path. He barely noticed the tiny creatures standing near the entrance.

"Halt! Who goes there?" the green bug called up to him.

Tusker turned to try to find the source of the voice. His eyes zoomed in on a tiny green bug with a few others next to him. He was a bright green color with an intricate spattering of red and black dots. Tusker let out a long sigh. He did not even bother answering him.

The bug waved his leg at Tusker. "I said halt!"

"Looks like he didn't hear you, Lenny," one of the other bugs snickered next to him.

"He's going to hear me just fine when I unleash my fury!" The bug seemed to shake with false bravado.

Tusker rolled his eyes at the insects. "There is not much you can do to me that I haven't already done to myself."

Tusker started to move forward again and the green bug shook his head. "You asked for it!"

As Tusker started to pass him, the bug let loose a stench unlike any Tusker had smelled before. He tucked his trunk into his mouth and tried to avoid it. This may have been comical to other animals, but to Tusker it was the last straw. He blew a gust of air from his trunk, knocking the bug from his perch. The other insects barely held on by their small prickly legs. Their fear made them tremble and lose control over their own smelly mechanisms. Tiny clouds of stink now permeated the air behind them.

"See what you made us do!" Their eyes were watering from the smell wafting around them.

"Oh! I think I'm going to be sick." One of them wavered slightly on the leaf before falling over backwards. He was knocked out cold from his own spray. The one next to him was dry heaving.

Tusker shook his head and continued on his way. As he entered the small valley, he let out a sad sigh.

"I've come home."

Tusker looked around him, comforted by the bones that littered the ground around him. He had lived a long life, and now it was time for him to release his worries once and for all. Too much grief surrounded him. He had allowed himself to fall into the dark cloud of sadness that had started the moment he had been captured. Up until that point, he had always felt like a gentle warrior, ready to take on the world. As he reflected on the elephants who were merely pawns, a tear started to leave his eyes. "What good am I?" Mentally and physically exhausted, Tusker allowed his body to fall to the ground.

A lone silhouette started to move toward him, and Tusker's weary eyes thought they glanced upon the Great Tusker himself. As it moved toward him, he saw that it was only Thunder. Tusker closed his eyes and ignored the soft shuffle of feet.

"What are you doing, Tusker?" Thunder's voice was calm, but there was worry hidden beneath it.

"Go away, lad." Tusker's mouth barely moved. He was ready for the Great Tusker to call him home.

"Is this why you wanted to come this direction?" Thunder gestured to the bones around him. Tears were filling his eyes.

"Never mind that. Just leave me be."

"Why, so you can die? How can you just give up like this after all of us risked our lives to save you?" Thunder's voice was filled with determination to shake his friend out of the hole he had dug himself into.

"I didn't ask for your help!" Tusker shouted at him. "I'm not worth it."

"Why do you think that? You are a legend to the rest of us."

"Legends are nothing but false hope. Our world doesn't need more of that." Tusker lifted his head slightly before dropping it back down. His body was so tired. He knew it was time for him to let go.

"Some hope is better than none. Do you think I would have come this far if I had given up?" Thunder stomped slightly on the ground, as his emotions were getting the best of him.

"Leave me be!" Tusker shouted at him.

Thunder sucked in his breath in shock. There was nothing he could do to save him in this moment in time. He had been there when his mother had died, but Thunder had been much younger and his anger against the injustice around him had forced him to keep going. Thunder knew that nothing he said would make a difference. Tusker had to find the strength inside of himself. "Suit yourself, old man."

As Thunder walked from the grave of bones, Tusker closed his eyes and breathed in the musky smell of the dirt around him. The cold fog of despair closed over him, and his lungs took in the shallow air around him.

A slight movement caught his attention, and Tusker opened his eyes. He saw a large shape coming closer to him, a dark moving body that blended in with the cloudy fog that rose from the ground. "I told you to leave me be!" When the elephant moved past the fog, Tusker's breath caught in his throat. "It's you!"

"I have always been with you." The Great Tusker in the sky was standing over him with a sadness reflected on his weary face.

"I'm not worthy of your time." Tusker looked away from him.

"But you are." The spirit put his trunk on Tusker's face and wiped away the tears that streamed down it. "Now is not the time for pity. Your life is not yet over. The world needs you."

"But what is the point of it all? They always win. I could not save them." Tusker closed his eyes and put his head back down on the ground.

"Sometimes it is not what we do that changes the world, but what we inspire others to do for themselves that makes the difference, Tusker. Your courage to leave brought a change you could not see. It grew inside them one petal at a time, until they made a choice to find courage within themselves." The Great Tusker waved his trunk in the air and an image formed in the clouds. Tusker saw Talulla leading the others in the opposite direction.

"What did she do?"

"She protected you. And in doing so, a strength started to grow. A strength she never knew she had inside. The uprights had always made sure her choices were of their making. Now, she is thinking for herself. You did that." The spirit smiled sadly at him. "Now, rise up, Tusker. You've got a lot more to do, I'm afraid."

"What can these weary bones do?" Tusker was still not ready to move.

"The sky is the limit when you have hope. The courage of the hundreds that have come before you beats in your heart still. I'm proud of you, Grandson."

Tusker felt the love pass from the spirit to himself. He rose slowly from the ground and looked his ancestor in the eyes. The guilt that he carried on his shoulders had been lifted, and Tusker felt lighter from being released from its burden. Knowing that his existence had changed the course of the others brought him comfort. As he stood there, he realized if he had given up it might have changed the path of another. "I will do better, Great Tusker."

"You already have." The spirit turned from him and started to walk back through the hazy mist. He disappeared almost as quickly as he had come.

Tusker walked from the valley of bones to where the others sat huddled together. Their faces were filled with sadness, as Thunder had told them that Tusker would not be returning to them. Tusker cleared his throat. "Uh…hem…. Why the long faces?"

Jabari launched himself at Tusker and wrapped his arms around his leg. "You're back!"

Tusker rubbed Jabari's back with his trunk. "I am."

Thunder's eyes met his. "Are you ready to continue?"

Tusker smiled at him. "I've still got a lot to do in this lifetime. A friend helped remind me."

Tusker gestured to the white cloud above them and Thunder smiled knowingly. "He is never far from us when we need him the most."

"Truer words were never spoken. Now, if you don't mind, I'd like to get as far away from this place as possible."

"Done," Thunder smiled.

The group welcomed Tusker back one at a time before they ate the food they had gathered. As soon as their bellies were full, they started back on their way. Their next destination would be Hope Haven, the safest place for endangered animals like them.

CHAPTER 16
CRONAN'S ATTACK!

Just beyond the valley, Cronan lay in wait with the cronies that were far too happy to do his bidding. Their loyalty was unquestionable. Each and every one of them would put their lives on the line for him. Why? Because Cronan was the biggest predator of all of them. This garnered him respect.

Sagara stood next to him. "So, what is the plan?"

"We wait for them to come out of the pass and attack." Cronan pointed to the sticks he had placed in the ground. The rocks around them represented their army of misfits. They were about twelve strong since all the wild dogs had joined them. It may not seem like much, but their ferocity made up for their size easily.

"And which do you go after first? The father or

daughter?" Sagara pointed to the smaller stick last.

"I don't know yet. If I kill Razor first, then Naya has to watch her father die. If I go for her, then he has to live with that pain." Cronan sprawled out on the ground and put his paw under his chin as he drew sketches in the dirt. He blew out of his mouth and the battle plan disintegrated. "Decisions, decisions."

"Either way, we end up with a full belly." Sagara's eyes lit up at the thought of feasting on their prey. They had not eaten fresh meat in quite some time. Banding up with Cronan was one of the smartest things any of them could have done. They would all dine well tonight.

Lyca came racing up to them. "So what's first?"

"Divide and conquer. Do you have the secret weapon?" Cronan asked Lyca.

"Yes, but I'm still not sure how this is supposed to keep the elephants from attacking us." Lyca held a piece of log in his hand. He had wrapped leaves around the opening at the top to keep its contents in place.

"Just do as you're told." Cronan's throat rumbled and Lyca cowered slightly.

"Yeah, stop questioning everything." Sagara shook his head at Lyca.

Lyca sneered at Sagara, baring his fangs up to his nose. He turned away from them, muttering to himself, then looked back at them. "I'll wait for the signal."

Sagara whispered to Cronan. "What's the signal again?"

"For the love of…." Cronan put his paw on his head and started to rub his temples. If these two did not get their act together, he would never have his revenge. All they had to do was separate the lions from the rest of the animals. "Look, they'll be here before you know it. Stay with your group and take care of the gorillas."

"On it!" Sagara raced away from Cronan and headed toward the others.

***

Now that Tusker had come back to them, the others were anxious to keep moving. They would have to pass through the Valley of the Bones that Tusker had just climbed out of. Thunder turned to Tusker. "If we go back in, will you still come back out?"

"Not to worry, my friend. The afterlife no longer clings to this soul. I'm ready to keep moving with this life." Tusker smiled at him. The sadness that had left him was starting to be replaced with a feeling he had not felt in quite some time…hope, mixed in with purpose. He had not realized that one action could revive the spirit deep inside him. There was still much to do.

"Good, because I would have found a way to carry you right back out," warned Salem.

"Why would you do that? You barely know me," Tusker pointed out.

"We didn't come all this way just to leave you behind, old man," Gamba called from overhead.

"Yeah…we believe in you." Thunder smiled at Tusker.

"I'm fortunate to have such wonderful friends." Tusker felt a warm glow fill his body.

Jabari scratched Thunder behind the ears. "I'm just lucky to have been here to see it."

As they started to cross through the valley, Kali started to sniff the air. "What is that smell?"

"Rotting bones?" Idi suggested.

"No…it's worse than that." Kali landed on the ground and started to sniff out the cause of the stench. When she saw the bugs grumbling on the ground, she tilted her head. "What are you?"

"Stink bugs, initiate!" Lenny stared up at her and clapped his front legs together. They all turned around so that their tail ends faced Kali.

She moved closer to them and tried to figure out what they were doing. "What are you little bugs doing? Are you going to put on a show?"

"Show? Ha, ha. We'll show her, boys! Now!"

As the bugs let loose another smoky steam of stink, Kali's expression changed from delight to absolute horror. She held one wing up to her mouth to block the stench, and used the other wing to wave it as far away as she could. This only ended up with her wafting it through her feathers and absorbing it into her fluff. She raced away from them, screaming and shaking her head in despair. "Oh my word! I just got stinked!"

"We can tell." Naya held a paw up to her nose as Kali zipped past.

Tusker chuckled slightly. "Yeah, I probably should have warned you about them."

"But then we would have missed this." Neville hooted as he watched Kali fly up into the air.

The group entered the Valley of the Bones with laughter in their hearts. As they continued the light started to shine down around them. Instead of the desolate world Tusker had walked through moments ago, he now saw the life growing around him. Where some animals had fallen, their lives had given back to the earth. Plants sprouted around the decay, and flowers blossomed from their stems. There was a peaceful beauty here. Often it was only by traveling through the darkness that one could see the life waiting on the other side.

No one said a word as they passed through the valley. It seemed the right thing to do, a respectful homage to the souls who lingered within its walls. When they reached the other side, the light continued to follow them. All seemed well until Razor stopped mid tracks.

"There is danger lurking nearby," he cautioned them.

Thunder turned to Harold and Neville. "I feel it too. You two take Jabari to safety. Protect him at all costs."

Harold nodded at him. "You got it. Come on down from there, boy."

"I don't want to go, Thunder. I want to stay and fight." Jabari made defiant fists in his lap.

"Live today so that you can fight for us another day," Tusker added.

Jabari slid down and walked over to Naya. He put his head against hers. "You better come back to me."

"As if you could get rid of me." She purred as she nuzzled her head against his.

They watched the gorillas take him back inside the valley. When they were sure Jabari was safe, the animals moved forward. The birds flew high into the sky to get a better view on the situation.

When Cronan rushed forward from the bush ahead of them, Razor leapt at him. The lions locked on each other with their legs, trying to gain access to each other with their sharp teeth. They rolled over the ground in vicious snarls.

A band of wild dogs came crashing through the brush. Salem, Thunder, and Tusker met them head on. They were about to toss them into the air when Lyca opened the log he had been cradling to his side. A large line of ants spilled from it, causing Tusker and Thunder to rise up on their back legs.

Salem looked at them as if they were crazy. "What is your problem?"

"ANTS!" Thunder almost squealed out of his trunk.

"Our tiniest foe!" Tusker was stomping the

ground everywhere he could, hoping to keep them off his feet.

"You have got to be kidding me!" Salem charged at the dogs, and several of them went flying into the air with loud yelps.

Lyca grabbed onto Salem's tail and was flapping behind him in the wind as Salem kept running. The dog kept banging into the ground and yelping every step of the way, but he refused to let go.

Naya saw the ants creeping closer to the elephants and raced over to them, quickly swiping them away. The tiny insects flew through the air, where they landed safely onto a rock ledge above them. One of them called back to her. "Thank you!"

"No problem." She turned to Thunder. "Time to do your thing!"

Thunder nodded at her. He pulled his legs into the air and pounded them against the ground as hard as he could. The ground shook from the strength of his booming thunder. The remaining dogs were rattled so much that they took off with a series of frightened yelps.

No one saw Sagara leap toward Naya. He landed on her neck and sunk his teeth into her fur. When he grabbed on, she shook him as hard as she could, but she could not break him free. The jackal growled as she rammed him into a rock. Nothing she did could break his hold.

Razor was still fighting Cronan. When he heard her painful wails, something snapped inside him. Even though he broke away from Cronan, he was not able to get to her. The lion had now attached himself to Razor's backside. His claws and teeth sunk into his flesh. Razor roared in pain.

A downpour of rocks came from the sky and a shriek caught Sagara's attention right before the eagle's talons sank into his flesh. The eagle may not have been as large as the jackal, but the adrenaline pumping through his veins would have let him move mountains. The bird hefted him into the air and carried him up as high as he could before releasing him back to the ground. The jackal fell to the ground with a loud yelp, and then was motionless.

At that moment, Naya launched herself at Cronan and knocked him off her father. Razor and Naya turned on Cronan, prepared to fight him together. The lion knew he had lost the battle. The coward he was showed on his face the moment before he decided to run. They could have followed after him, but that served no real purpose. It was less than likely that Cronan would attack them again.

The rest of them gathered around the lions. Thunder looked at them with concern. "Are you all right?"

Razor licked a few of his wounds and grinned at him. "I've had worse."

Naya launched herself at him and pinned him to the ground. She swatted at his face a few times. "I thought he was going to kill you!"

Razor chuckled and pushed her off him. "I'm fine. And if your mother asks, this never happened."

Naya shook her head at her father. "Men!"

"You tell 'em, girlfriend!" Kali called down to her.

The group laughed collectively as they tried to settle their beating hearts. "Well...now that we've tackled that, should we continue on?" suggested Tusker.

"Right. We've got to get you back to Thandi." Gamba, who had landed on the ground, looked up at Tusker.

"Nicely done, Gamba," Tusker said to him.

Gamba blushed. "It was nothing."

"Courage is never to be frowned upon, Gamba. You are more than enough, my friend."

Gamba puffed out his chest in pride. "That is the best compliment anyone can have."

"What's that?" Tusker asked him.

"Your friendship."

"All right. Stop the love fest already. It's time to get moving, before those animals come back." Salem cut through it. The rhino was having trouble keeping the moisture out of his eyes at such a display.

"Right. Onward!" Neville held up his hand and pointed them onward. Jabari climbed up onto Thunder's back and the group continued their journey. They were half way to Hope Haven, where Tusker would be safe at last.

CHAPTER 17
THAT KID IS IN TROUBLE

Not too far away from the entourage of animals, another foe lay in wait. The poacher lay on his stomach and held a pair of binoculars up to his eyes. Cayman turned to Berko and waved him closer. "Look! There they are. If we keep pushing forward, we'll catch up to them."

Berko nodded his head. "And what will we do when we do?"

"What do you mean, Berko?" Cayman looked at his friend like he was addled.

"Well, before it was just that tusker. Now there's two elephants, a rhino, and some gorillas. Might as well throw in a pear tree while we're at it."

"Ah, ye of little faith, Berko."

"I have plenty of faith, Cayman, but it doesn't always put food on the table." Berko sat next to him. "Are you sure we should do this? There's only two of us…and well, those there."

Cayman glanced at the elephants that stood trembling nearby. "They're still of use to us. Especially now that I've brought Talulla back around."

Talulla shook at the sound of her name. She had a few scars on her backside for her defiance earlier. When Cayman had realized that she was leading him in the wrong direction, he had taken it out on her. The others were now more afraid of what would happen if they ever went against his orders again. Cayman had never been that angry before.

Cayman sat up and let the binoculars slide around his neck. "We'll hit them before they get to the refuge."

"Good. I don't want to mess with Hope Haven." Berko's eyes grew wide at the thought of facing off with the men and women who protected the animals near Hope Haven.

"I don't relish the idea either." Cayman did not want to mess with Hope Haven at all if he could avoid it. The organization had grown over the years. What used to be a small encampment had now grown into a stretch of land that was formidable. The more press they got, the more power they seemed to have. They were one of the reasons that Cayman had started capturing animals alive. The fines for killing an elephant for its ivory were far steeper than a live capture. It was easier to plead innocence when they pretended to be saving them and releasing them to a safer area. Besides, Cayman knew a few collectors who wanted the animals for their own private zoos. Money could buy almost anything, if someone had enough of it.

"How long do you think it will take us?" Berko asked him.

"If we move now, we can meet up with them before the end of the day. Get the elephants together," Cayman ordered.

Berko nodded at him and stepped to the elephants. They cowered when he neared them. Pace turned to Talulla. "How do you suppose two uprights are going to get Tusker away from all of those animals?"

"I don't know, Pace. Greed is blinding," Talulla whispered to him. Small tears fell from her eyes as Berko used his whip against her wounds.

"Move it, Talulla," Berko ordered. The other elephants fell in line right behind her.

Cayman lifted his binoculars one last time. This time he spotted the boy traveling with them. "What have we here?"

"What?" Berko asked him.

"That boy is running around with those animals. How is that possible?" Cayman was surprised. "Those animals would never let us get close enough to them. How did that boy manage it?"

"Let me see." Berko grabbed the binoculars and looked through them. "Is he talking to them?"

"He must be out of his mind, that one." Cayman shook his head and laughed.

"No...I don't think so. Look, they are gathering around him." Berko handed the binoculars back.

"I think you're right. Is that...?"

"Jabari?" Berko supplied. His name was known around Africa as the boy who could speak to animals. His mother, Imani, had practically built Hope Haven from the ground up.

"That kid is trouble," Cayman swore.

"Unless...."

"What are you thinking, Berko?" Cayman turned to face him.

"Well, if we control the boy, we could control the

animals, right?"

"You may be on to something, Berko." Cayman slapped him on the shoulder and nodded his head.

Pace turned to Talulla. "Did you hear that?"

"I did. But what can we do about it?" Talulla looked away. Her heart was weary. Having used the only ounce of courage she had, she was less likely to do it again. The three elephants traveled across the distance, their eyes reflecting the hopelessness that they had come to be used to over the course of the years.

***

When the group of animals came to a stop, they started to forage for food. Now that they had put enough distance between them and the Valley of Bones, they felt much safer. Thunder turned to Tusker. "Do you want to dig or should I?"

"I got it. Besides, these tusks are much stronger." Tusker started to root in the dirt.

The gorillas were being groomed by the egrets, who were sucking up the bugs greedily. Harold chuckled. "Nothing like a personal groomer."

"I do say, where have they been all our lives?" Neville sneezed when a feather tickled his nose.

Jabari giggled at them. "Next thing you know, Thunder will be blow drying you."

Thunder gave them a half-grin. "That can be arranged."

Jabari stood up. "Did you hear that?"

"What?" Thunder turned to him.

"Nothing. I must be imagining things. I think I'm going to go look for some fruit." Jabari turned away from them.

"Be careful, Jabari," Thunder warned him.

"Oh, don't worry about me. I can take care of myself." He grinned up at Thunder. "Besides, those animals aren't coming back, and I can talk my way out of almost anything."

Jabari walked away from the group to where he thought he'd heard an animal calling out for help. When he found a small painted African dog, he approached the animal slowly. The dog struggled against the small trap that was keeping him held to the ground. The more he struggled the more pain it caused him. Jabari held his hand up. "Relax, I'm here to help."

"You try relaxing with jaws of death clamped over your leg," the dog bit out.

"I would probably be more afraid than you are. You're very brave," Jabari soothed him.

The dog whimpered slightly. "Do you think so?"

"Of course I do. Can I take this off you?"

"Please…." The dog was in awe of the upright boy. He had never seen one that could understand them before.

Jabari found a stick and a rock nearby. He used the stick to pry open the trap, and when the jaws were almost away from the dog's leg, he put the large rock inside it to keep it from clamping back down on it.

The dog moved his leg out as quickly as he could manage. When he stood up, he used his three good legs to balance himself. It was then that the dog realized who Jabari had traveled with, as Naya came out of the brush with a growl on her face.

"Get away from him!" Naya warned the dog.

"I mean him no harm," the dog answered. He stepped back and dropped his head as if to bow toward Jabari.

"You were there with the others," accused Naya. "I can smell their stench on you."

The dog stepped back a few steps. "We didn't mean anything…."

Naya was prepared to leap at him, but Jabari put a hand on her neck. "Stop Naya. The world does not need more violence. Let him go."

Naya turned up to Jabari and nodded at him. "I'll let him go so he can fight another day."

The dog moved away as quickly as his injury would allow him. Naya moved into the brush behind him. Jabari called out to her. "Where are you going?"

"To make sure he leaves." Naya smiled at him. "Don't worry. I won't touch him."

"I trust you, Naya." Jabari chuckled as he watched her go. He had little time to reflect on the encounter, for a voice called out to him.

"So, the great whisperer." Cayman sneered at him. "I see you've taken our elephant."

"You can't take what doesn't belong to you." Jabari stood up and put his hands on his hips in defiance.

"Sure you can. I do it all the time. And now, we're going to take you." Cayman flashed a sharp smile.

"No you wo—"

His words were cut off by the hand that was place over his mouth. A strong arm wrapped around him and pulled him close. Jabari jerked his body as hard as he could, trying to release himself, but the man's strength outweighed his own.

"Tie him up and throw him on one of the elephants," Cayman ordered the man.

The elephants, seeing the way the young boy was treated, were starting to whisper among themselves.

"We can't let them take that boy. He tried to save us," Lala reminded them. She was the smaller of the three, the one who rarely acted out. But seeing the boy so defenseless was like another reminder of the cruelty of the world around them.

"She's right, Talulla. We have to stand up for him." Pace held his trunk up and the other two reached for it.

"On three…we raise as much noise as we can. The others can't be that far away from here."

As Berko forced Jabari closer, Pace whispered to him. "Relax, we've got your back, little one."

Jabari's eyes lit up. He would have answered him, but the man still had his mouth covered. Instead he wiggled his eyelids up and down.

"Be ready to run, do you understand?"

Jabari's eyes flashed at them. He did not want the elephants to come to any harm. They seemed to understand his fear.

"Don't worry. We'll be fine. Besides, we've already called Thunder." Talulla pointed to her feet with her trunk. "Ready?"

As Berko brought him toward the elephants, a flurry of action happened in an instant. Pace went back on his back legs and kicked Berko in the side. The man fell to the ground, and Jabari rolled with him. When Berko released his hold, Jabari took off to where he had last seen Naya, knowing that the lion would keep him safe.

Cayman turned to the elephants with anger plastered across his face. He held up the electrified prod that he always carried with him and came over to them. "Now you're going to get it."

"And so are you," trumpeted Talulla. The three of them started toward him, prepared to trample over him, when a loud roar came from behind him.

Razor, Salem, Thunder, and the gorillas had joined them. In his fear, Cayman dropped his stick. He shrieked in fear and stepped back. "Run, Berko!"

Berko had no trouble following that order, especially since Harold had picked up the stick and activated its switch. Electricity crackled from its tip as the gorilla stepped closer to Cayman. If the upright had not started to run for his life, he might have had a taste of his own medicine.

Thunder turned to the elephants and bowed his head. "Thank you for keeping Jabari safe. That took a lot of courage."

"It was nothing," Talulla answered him.

Tusker now entered the clearing. He cleared his throat. "It was everything."

"Indeed," Thunder agreed. "Please, join us."

Talulla looked over at the other two. "I think we shall."

They made their way back to where the rest of their group waited. Jabari was seated next to Naya with a big smile on his face when he saw the other three elephants were now with them. "That was brilliant!"

"And stupid," Thunder chided him. "Your mother would have my hide if she knew I let you get in harm's way."

Jabari chuckled. "She would never take a hide. Besides, I am *her* child. She kind of expects it."

Thunder shook his head. "It's time to get moving again. We're almost there."

CHAPTER 18
LYCA'S REDEMPTION

Cronan's rage knew no bounds. The more he thought about the lions, the more he fumed. He looked at them frolicking now with the upright that seemed to have brought them together. Naya was quite fond of him. If he were to strike a big enough blow, taking out the boy, his anger would be soothed slightly.

Turning to Lyca, he waved him over. "Do you see that boy there?"

Lyca looked down at him and sniffed the air slightly. "Yes."

"We need to take him down."

"Why do we need to do that?" Lyca asked him.

Cronan let out a roar of rage. "Do not question

me, you fool!"

Lyca yelped and stepped back with his head bowed. "Yes, Cronan."

"You're now my first in command."

"But Sagara—"

"Knew what he was getting into the minute he joined up with me. If you had half the courage he did, you would be a worthy companion. I'm stuck with you until I can find someone better, it seems." Cronan looked down at his paws and shook the dirt from the crevices.

Lyca sneered behind Cronan's back, but he dared not utter his disapproval of his leader's actions. "What do you want me to do?"

"Gather the others. It's the only thing you're good at." Cronan rolled his eyes in disgust.

Lyca bowed his head and moved away from the lion to search for the other wild dogs that made up his pack. When he found them, they were surrounding one of the others. "What's going on?"

"The boy who speaks…the whisperer…," one of them answered.

"What about him?" Lyca's ears perked up as he stepped closer.

"He saved me." The injured dog who had been caught in the trap was now sitting among the others. "He could have left me there."

"The boy saved you?" Lyca felt his heart sink to the bottom of his stomach. How could they take down someone who had put himself at risk to save one of their kind? The boy did not have to do that.

"He did. Even kept the lioness from attacking me, if you can believe that."

"Why would she do that?" Lyca was perplexed, and that was saying a lot for his half-brained self.

"Because he bridges the gap between all of us?" suggested one of them.

"But Cronan wants us to take him out." Lyca clasped his paw to his mouth after the words left his mouth.

"He wants us to do what?" one of the dogs asked him.

"He thinks the lioness is attached to him. If we kill him off, it will feed his revenge." Lyca waved his paw in the air matter of factly.

"We shall see about that," another dog sniffed in irritation.

"Look, to go against him would be crazy. And I

know crazy, don't get me wrong. I'm just not sure it's in our best interest." Lyca waved his paw in the air as if to illustrate his thoughts.

"Standing up for others never is...but in the end we are better for it." The injured dog stood up and nodded for them to come closer. "This is what we do...."

***

Later that day, Jabari hung back from the other animals. He knew that he would be home soon, and he was not ready to return. When he had snuck off, his mother had been quite angry at him. Jabari had accidentally set some of the animals free from their pens. In his defense, though, the animals had begged him to do so. Jabari had a hard time not helping an animal that was looking at him with sad eyes.

Jabari sighed. If the animals had not wreaked havoc on the food supply, it might have gone better for him. Imani had yelled at him until she was nearly blue in the face. He had never seen her so angry before. That night he had slipped off and run into the darkness. He had run as fast and far as his legs would carry him. Days had passed before he realized that he was lost.

"What's wrong, Jabari?" Kali flew down and

perched on the limb above him.

"I'm afraid to go home."

"You afraid?" Kali's eyes rose in surprise. "I didn't think you were afraid of anything."

"I made a mistake and my mother got mad at me."

"I see. Well…it's better to face the music, I always say. And I've had symphonies made for all the times I've messed up, if you can believe it."

Jabari smiled up at the flamingo and flashed his bright teeth. "You? Trouble? Never."

"Pshaw! I'm not always this fantastic." Kali gestured to herself. "When I need a break, though, I usually get sent to my Uncle Frederick. He doesn't seem to mind my shade of crazy."

"I don't mind it either, Kali. It looks good on you." Jabari reached his hand up and scratched the flamingo on her neck. He still could not figure out why she was up in the tree instead of the ground, but it was her strangeness that made her so endearing.

"Aww. You're going to make me blush, and I don't care what Uncle Freddie says, red clashes with pink! Blech!" Kali stepped away and jumped back into the air.

"Well, wasn't that a lovely little scene." Cronan's voice was dripping with malice.

"What do you want?" Jabari held his hand up in front of him. "I'll call my friends."

"They won't be of much help to you, I'm afraid." Cronan was about to launch himself at Jabari, but a flash of fur leapt through the sky.

Naya rammed into him and the two rolled on the ground. The next few moments were filled with flashing teeth and slashing claws as the two lions fought for dominance. This was not the fight it had been before. Each one was out for blood. When Cronan got the advantage over Naya, he used his might to fling her through the air. Naya landed hard against a rock and her body slumped on the ground.

"I got you just where I want you," Cronan laughed maniacally. He started toward Naya, but Jabari leapt in front of her.

"Stop! I won't let you hurt her." Jabari held his ground with his hands up in small fists.

"Who's going to stop me? You? Your time is short. Get him!" he roared to the dogs behind the rock.

The dogs came as beckoned, but instead of tearing into the boy, they surrounded him and started to snarl at Cronan.

The lion roared again. "What are you fools doing? Kill him."

"No...." Lyca stood in front of him and held his ground. He threw his head back and howled louder than any wolf ever could. His pack around him joined in the chorus.

"Fine! I'll do it myself." Cronan jumped into the air, his eyes flashing with anger.

The dogs leapt into action. One of them pushed Jabari behind them and blocked him from the attack. "Stay back."

Jabari knelt down next to Naya and held on tight. He squeezed his eyes shut as he heard the snarls and slashes behind him. He was prepared to be mowed down when he heard a crunch of bones before everything went still. Standing up, he looked to where the dogs were grouped. In a matter of moments, the whole pack had taken down the unsuspecting lion. Cronan now lay motionless on the ground.

Jabari closed his eyes and shook his head. Another death of a beautiful creature, even though this one hid his ugliness deep inside. Death was still that, a loss. Jabari turned back to Naya and sat down next to her. He wrapped his arms around her neck and started to sob into her neck, all the while praying for a miracle.

"Do you mind? You're getting snot all over my fur," Naya whispered to him.

"Naya!!" He hugged her tight.

"Ouch...ouch...okay, okay...not so hard. I'd like to breathe." Naya struggled to sit up. The dogs walked over to her and helped her to her feet. She regarded them with respect and nodded at them. "Our fight is over."

"Yes. It is," Lyca answered.

Jabari turned to the wild dog and bowed his head. "You were braver than the strongest wolf. Your pack should be proud."

Lyca's chest puffed out in pride. For once, he felt the call of the wild racing through him. His bumbling youth he could not change, but his future would never be the same. "We've much to do, boys."

The dogs turned away from them and trotted off into the distance. Jabari looked away from the crumpled lion and started his way back to the others. Having lived through this attack, Jabari was not nearly as afraid of his mother. In fact, all he could think about was hugging her tight and never letting go. Life was too precious.

CHAPTER 19
PINS AND NEEDLES

Razor was on pins and needles by the time Jabari had returned to the group. He had heard his daughter's roar, but by the time he made his way to her, she was already limping away. "What happened?"

"Justice." Naya held her head high. "We'll not be bothered by the likes of him anymore."

"Are you all right, daughter?" Razor asked her.

"Of course. I take after my father, after all." She nodded to the slight gash on her side. She was limping from the pain, but she pushed herself forward.

"Mom will fix her right up," Jabari added with a smile.

"I'm sure she will." Razor smiled at him. "Let's

169

keep moving."

They moved with the group until they reached the outskirts of the preserve where the injured animals were kept. Tusker stopped in his tracks when he heard a familiar rumble. "Stop." They all stopped moving and Tusker shifted his legs over the ground. His ears flapped excitedly. "It's Thandi!"

Thunder smiled at him. "See...just as Gamba said."

Gamba swooped down from the sky and landed at Tusker's feet. He looked up at the gentle giant. "It's been a pleasure assisting you, my friend."

"I wouldn't have had it any other way, Gamba." Tusker turned to his friends. "I'm sure I will see you around. There's much to do still, but for now my heart calls me home."

"I understand," Thunder nodded to him.

"Goodbye for now." Tusker turned from them and headed toward Thandi, who was grazing nearby with her herd.

Jabari patted Naya softly on her side. "Come on, girl. Let's get you fixed up."

Jabari led her through the wooden gates that separated Hope Haven from the outside world. As they made their way through them a loud scream echoed from one of the huts. "Jabari!!"

"Uh-oh…," Jabari gulped. It was time for him to find out how much trouble he was in.

Imani came racing from the hut. She flung her arms around her son and lifted him off the ground. Spinning around, she hugged him tight. "My boy! I was so worried!!!"

"I'm sorry, Mother." Jabari sniffed slightly as he held her tight.

"Oh, my dear boy. Food can be replaced, but you, my son, you are irreplaceable." Imani turned to look at the crowd of animals around her. She was filled with awe. "What do we have here?" Thunder stepped closer to her and held up his trunk to greet her. A tear fell from her eye. "Of course, my old friend. Thank you, Thunder. For bringing my child home to me."

The gorillas had not come inside the gates. They were happy to watch the reunion from a distance. Imani nodded to them. When she saw Tusker racing across the field, her breath caught in her throat. "A tusker! How can that be?"

"The world works in mysterious ways, doesn't it?" Jabari smiled.

"That it does, my boy. That it does. Who is this?"

Imani looked down at the lioness who stood next to Jabari.

"This is Naya. You already know Razor. This is his cub." Jabari pointed to the other lion.

"Oh goodness! Look at you, old man!" Imani was impressed with how healthy the lion appeared. "You certainly didn't waste any time, did you? Where's Sasha?"

"I don't know. She wasn't with him. I imagine she is with another litter?" Jabari smiled at Razor, who beamed proudly.

"Well, it's quite the reunion. Speaking of which, I think someone is here for you too, Thunder." Imani gestured to the tree line nearby.

Thunder looked to where she pointed and heard a call just for him. "Kumani!"

Razor turned to him. "I wonder what she's doing here?"

Thunder turned to Imani and nuzzled her with his trunk.

"It's okay, my friend. Go to her. I've got someone to patch up here, anyway."

Jabari knelt down to Naya. "Mom will take good care of you. Let's go."

Thunder heard another call for him and turned back to the sound. "Something's wrong."

"You better go. We'll be fine here."

Thunder raced across the field, as fast as his feet would carry him. He found Kumani weeping by a tree. Her belly jerked in reflex as the calf within pushed against it.

"What's wrong, Kumani?"

"Oh, Thunder! I tried to keep him safe, but he just got it in his head that he had to prove how brave he was."

"Where is Junior?" Thunder felt his heart sink.

"He went to find you, and before I knew it, the uprights came. I couldn't keep up with them, Thunder." Her voice cracked as a bitter sadness wrapped through her.

Thunder put his head on hers and a tear left his eyes. "Quiet, my love. This is the moment I've always dreaded, but remember that even in the midst of despair, hope can survive."

"What if they kill him?"

"He's made of stronger stuff than most other animals. And we have taught him everything we know. We've both survived this, Kumani. He will too. He has to." Thunder stood as tall as his legs would let him. Right now, hope was the only thing they had to hang onto. He was not about to let go of it.

Kali flew down from the trees. She saw the sadness in their faces. "What's wrong?"

"My son is missing."

"Don't worry, I'm sure you'll find him soon." Kali landed on the ground, and for the first time acted like a flamingo. She lifted one leg and stood on the other as she hugged Thunder's leg. "You just have to have hope." Kali's eyes jerked open wider and she started to shake her head in a bizarre fashion. "Hey! That tickles!"

Kali lifted her pilot's hat and a blue butterfly flew into the air. Katerina had been with them the other time. The pudgy little caterpillar had turned into something so beautiful it took all their breaths away.

"Jennetta Blue?" Thunder whispered as he recalled his friend from long ago.

"It's Katerina…Katerina Blue, thank you very much." The beautiful butterfly flew in tentative circles before landing on Thunder's head. Though his heart was heavy, he felt peace through him. He knew that everything was going to be okay. Someday, his family would be reunited. Until then, Thunder would make sure their new calf came into this world surrounded by all the animals who had been his family for as long as he could remember.

Katerina Blue fluttered her striking wings and flew into the air. They watched her until she faded from sight, knowing that there were many stories left to write. The fight to bring peace to their world was affirmed with the rolling white clouds that slowly formed above them. The face of the Great Tusker smiled down on them, reassuring them that all was not lost.

About the Author

Erik Daniel Shein was born Erik Daniel Stoops, November 18th 1966. He is an American writer and visionary, film producer, screenwriter, voice actor, animator, entrepreneur, entertainer and philanthropist, pet enthusiast and animal health advocate. He is the author and co-author of over thirty nonfiction and fiction books, whose writings include six scientific articles in the field of herpetology. His children's book, "The Forgotten Ornament" is a Christmas classic, and was endorsed by Hollywood legends Mickey and Jan Rooney.

Author credits: Animated Film "The Legend of Secret Pass"
https://www.youtube.com/watch?v=SPUJy2DYRZw
http://www.imdb.com/title/tt0765465/combined
http://www.malcolminthemiddle.co.uk/2007/06/20/frankie-muniz-the-legend-of-secret-pass-movie/

About the Author

Born in Southern Illinois, Melissa Davis fell in love with reading from an early age, so much so that she started writing when she was in the second grade. From poetry to short stories, she has a love for it all. When she was in high school she attended Illinois Summer School for the Arts at Illinois State University, which led her to attend the university. After graduating with a Bachelors in Education, Melissa taught for several years until her children were born, allowing her to fulfill two dreams at once: motherhood and penning her first books.

CPSIA information can be obtained
at www.ICGtesting.com
Printed in the USA
LVOW12*1941160418

573652LV00007B/113/P